BOOK TWO: CARRION

BLACK SWAN

MARK GOODWIN

Technical information in the book is included to convey realism. The author shall not have liability or responsibility to any person or entity with respect to any loss or damage caused, or allegedly caused, directly or indirectly by the information contained in this book.

All of the characters, places, and incidents are products of the author's imagination or are used fictitiously. Any resemblance to actual people, places, or events is entirely coincidental.

Copyright © 2019 Goodwin America Corp.

All rights reserved. No part of this publication may be reproduced, stored in a retrieval system, or transmitted in any form or by any means without the prior written permission of the author, except by a reviewer who may quote short passages in a review.

ISBN: 9781086420708

ACKNOWLEDGMENTS

All glory, and honor, and praise to the King of Kings, Jesus Christ who has saved me from myself, paid my debt, and has blessed me beyond my wildest dreams.

I would like to thank my Editor in Chief Catherine Goodwin, as well as the rest of my fantastic editing team, Jeff Markland, Frank Shackleford, Stacey Glemboski, Sherrill Hesler, and Claudine Allison.

CHAPTER 1

Man that is born of a woman is of few days and full of trouble. He cometh forth like a flower, and is cut down: he fleeth also as a shadow, and continueth not.

Job 14:1-2

Two months after the collapse of the US Dollar.

Shane Black sank the spade of the shovel deep into the dark earth. He glanced over at Julianna working the dirt down the row from him. The way she looked in her denim overalls made his heart flutter. Shane quickly turned his attention to his father before Julianna caught him staring. "That should keep everything from washing into the creek if we get a downpour. But anything we plant in this last row isn't going to get much drainage."

Paul Black inspected the raised ridge of dirt running along the bottom edge of the garden plot. "I'm more worried about having all my topsoil washed away than I am about flooding this bottom row. I meant to have this meadow leveled out. I guess that's what I get for procrastinating."

"I've seen plenty of gardens on a steeper grade than this do just fine." Pastor Joel leaned on the wooden handle of his hoe.

Julianna broke up some leftover clods of dirt with the metal rake. "I've never heard of anyone around here putting in a garden in mid-March. Most people don't plant until Mother's Day."

"We could still get frost in the next two months, but we're only putting in the things that can handle it. Peas, cabbage, and root vegetables, they'll all do fine even if we get a few cold nights." Paul handed a package of beet seeds to Shane. "An early crop will go a long way in stretching out our supplies."

Bobby's voice came over the walkie-talkie. "We've got a law enforcement vehicle turning into the drive."

Shane tucked the packet in his shirt pocket and retrieved his radio from his belt. "Ask Dan if he knows who it is."

Dan Ensley's voice came back. "I think it's Deputy Bivens."

Paul took Shane's radio and pressed the talk key. "Eric Bivens? Let him through if he's alone."

"Roger Dodger," said Dan.

Shane and the others watched as the sheriff's department patrol car rolled to a halt on the gravel drive above the garden plot. Deputy Bivens exited his vehicle and walked down to where Shane and the others stood.

"Good morning," said the deputy as he approached.

"Eric, good to see you." Paul embraced the deputy's hand. "To what do we owe the pleasure?"

Bivens looked at the dirt as if evading Paul's gaze. "Hand delivering a letter from the county commissioners."

Paul took the envelope and began opening it. "You don't look proud to be carrying the news. Should I be worried?"

Bivens pressed his lips together. "It is what it is, Mr. Black. It's probably not the way I would have handled it, but the Jackson County commissioners have their backs against the wall. Since it doesn't look like this gold dollar is going to work out, they have to do something."

"Special assessment tax, due June 1st." Paul's face soured as he began reading. "I don't suppose Mayor Hayes had a hand in putting this together."

"The mayor has no say in affairs of the county, Paul." Deputy Bivens let his hands rest with his thumbs tucked inside his ballistic vest. "We have to fund the government. I love my job, but I gotta eat. We've lost over half of our guys since this all started. Sylva PD is down to about four officers. All the fire departments in the county have consolidated to Sylva. They can still respond if it's a catastrophic fire unless it's in Highlands. They're so far out, the trucks would never get there in time to save anything, so the protocol for Highlands is let it burn.

"Not to mention the hospital. Insurance companies, Medicare, Medicaid, they're all belly-up. If we want to keep the skeleton staff we have, which is currently one surgeon, one ER doctor, and about seven nurses, the county has to figure out a way to fund it."

"I don't have any problem taking care of you folks, but you know as well as I do that this is going to get siphoned off by Wallace Hayes and his cronies." Paul held out the letter to the deputy. "They're asking for a tenth-ounce of gold, ten ounces of silver, or the barter equivalent to $1,000 in goods based on pre-crash prices. That's not per farm. That's for every man, woman, and child.

"And my share? $50,000!" Paul wadded up the letter and threw it into the middle of the garden plot. "I don't have 50 people living here!"

Bivens watched the wrinkled tax bill land between the furrows like a roulette ball. "You wouldn't fill out the census. The commission had to come up with their own number. You knew they were going to go high with the estimate." Bivens stepped out into the field and retrieved the crinkled form. He smoothed it out and refolded it. "Why don't you ask for a new census form and request that the board reassess your bill?" He gave the letter back to Paul. They'll foreclose on anyone who hasn't paid by August 1st."

"Caesar better be careful, trying to dismantle the republic and replace it with a totalitarian empire, especially this being the Ides of March and all." Pastor Joel took the letter from Paul to look over.

Deputy Bivens seemed to catch the historical reference. His brow creased. "Since you're the mayor's brother, I'm going to pretend I didn't hear that, Pastor Joel."

"Do what you like, Eric." Pastor Joel passed the letter to Shane to examine. "But We the People are still calling the shots. You best make sure of what side you want to be on when this thing comes to a head."

The deputy looked Shane, Paul, and Pastor Joel in their eyes, as if studying their resolve. Even Julianna joined them with gazes set like flint, unwavering in standing their ground. Bivens nodded ever so slightly. "Y'all take care." He returned to his patrol car and drove away.

"Do you think he'll side with us?" Shane asked.

"Eric is a good kid." Paul stuck the crumpled letter in his back pocket. "He'll do the right thing."

"You said We the People are in control." Julianna held the metal rake upright. "Exactly how do you see us exercising that control?"

Pastor Joel looked at Paul. "We've spoken to all the neighbors and folks from church. They've all helped to spread the word. We were anticipating something like this. When we mentioned taking a stand, hypothetically, about ninety percent of the people we talked to were behind us. I expect several will fall away since it's no longer hypothetical, but we'll still have a strong majority."

"Majority for what?" she asked.

"Cutting the head off the snake," Paul replied.

"Mayor Hayes being the snake. How will you pull that off?" She shifted her weight to lean against the rake.

"We'll get him to the property and detain him until the federal government is back up and running. Then, we can have him charged for extortion." Pastor Joel's answer was sharp and swift.

Julianna nodded. "Right, as if either of those things are likely to happen."

"We may have to take a rain check on the government, but my brother is always the politician. We can get him to the property." The pastor sounded confident.

"How do we do that?" Shane inquired.

The pastor looked to Paul. "Have a public shindig. Invite lots of people. He'll see it as an opportunity to shake hands, kiss babies, and convince everyone that, while he hates it just as much as anyone else, the city and the county have no other choice than to enforce this onerous tax."

Shane gave a lopsided smile. "No one can afford shindigs of any kind. Especially the sort that might lure the mayor."

"People still get together for important events," Paul countered.

"Yeah, for weddings and funerals." Julianna seemed to be losing faith in the scheme. "And for a funeral, you need a dead body."

"But not for a wedding," the pastor rebutted.

"You can't base your entire plan around the mayor showing up for some random wedding." Shane shook his head.

"No, but if it were a celebrity wedding, you can

bet your bottom dollar he'd be there," said Pastor Joel.

"With bells on," agreed Paul.

Shane caught the way the two were looking at him. "I'll play the part, but I don't know who you'd use for my fictitious bride. I haven't left the property more than a handful of times since I came back from Nashville. Anyone you find isn't going to be very believable."

Pastor Joel and Paul simultaneously turned their attention to Julianna.

It seemed to take her a second to understand the implication of their stares. "What? Are you serious?" Her confusion quickly turned to anger. Her face reddened, erasing the faint freckles on her cheeks which normally stood out in contrast to her smooth, milky complexion. "Absolutely not!" She set her teeth together in a vicious snarl and turned to Shane as if to accuse him of conspiring with his father and the pastor. Her brows sank down heavily against her eyelids and she reiterated her objection directly to Shane. "Absolutely not!"

"It would just be a ruse to get the mayor here. We're not asking you to do anything." The pastor held his hands up as one might do to a bear with its paw reared back for a fatal strike.

"You wouldn't even have to leave your trailer that day," Paul assured her. "It's not customary for the bride to be seen until she comes down the aisle anyway. We'd have the mayor in custody by then."

She glared at Shane as if this were all his fault. Her chin wrinkled as if she were about to cry. She hurled the metal rake in Shane's direction, missing his leg only because he stepped back in the nick of time. "Say whatever you have to say, but don't expect me to like it. Not even the pretense of marrying Shane Black is *remotely* acceptable to me." She stomped across the freshly plowed dirt toward her trailer. "I guess I should look on the bright side. I can pretend this is my chance to leave *him* standing at the altar."

Shane felt the words cut deeper than the jagged blade of a Mayan obsidian knife. Determined to not let his father and the pastor see him break down in tears, Shane quickly gathered the gardening tools and left. "I'll get these back to the garage."

CHAPTER 2

Brethren, I count not myself to have apprehended: but this one thing I do, forgetting those things which are behind, and reaching forth unto those things which are before, I press toward the mark for the prize of the high calling of God in Christ Jesus.

Philippians 3:13-14

Shane kicked the dirt off of his boots on the deck of the main cabin, but still did not venture inside. "Cole, come on. Let's go see if we can catch something for dinner."

The six-year-old boy had been busy helping Tonya Black cut out biscuits. "Okay!"

Tonya helped the young lad down from the chair he'd been standing on. She kissed him on the head. "You catch a big one and Grandma Black will make you a little treat for dessert."

He smiled as if enjoying the affection. "I will. I'll get one this big!" He held his hands far apart.

Shane chided his mother with stern eyes over her new self-appointed title.

"Dan Ensley's boy calls me Grandma Black, also." She placed the biscuits on the metal sheet pan. "Don't worry, I won't let the cat out of the bag." She wouldn't look in Shane's direction but seemed to be suppressing a mischievous grin.

"We'll see you later." Shane took Cole's hand and closed the door behind them.

"Scott's daddy is on guard duty. You don't mind if Scott comes fishing with us, do you?" Shane led the way down the drive to the basement garage of the main cabin where the fishing poles were stored.

"Scott can come. But I get the red fishing pole."

Shane smiled. "That sounds like a deal."

The two of them gathered the gear and continued to the upper clearing where the trailers were. Shane knocked softly on the Ensleys' trailer door, not wanting to alert Julianna to his presence since she lived in the last trailer on the row.

Kari came to the door. "Hey, Shane."

"Hi, I told Dan that I'd take Scott fishing."

"Scott, want to go fishing with Shane and Cole?"

"Yeah!" The seven-year-old boy rushed to the door and put on his boots.

Kari kissed her son. "You be good and obey Shane."

"I will. Bye!" Scott took the pole offered to him by Shane and ran ahead.

Cole took off after him.

Shane waved at Kari. "See you later. I've gotta get moving if I want to keep up." Shane jogged to maintain pace with the youngsters.

Once at the pond, he placed lures on each of their poles. The two boys made a great time of casting and reeling in their bobbers.

An hour later Julianna came to the pond. "Cole, come on baby. It's time to come home."

Cole shook his head. "We gotta go eat at Grandma Black's tonight. She's making me a special dessert."

"Grandma Black?" Julianna, who'd previously seemed oblivious to Shane's presence, suddenly turned to him with glaring eyes and flared nostrils.

Shane took a step back and held up one palm. "Scott calls her Grandma Black, too."

"Mama! Mama! Look!" Cole pointed at Sorghum, Mrs. Perkins' tabby, who was getting a drink from the edge of the pond.

Julianna exhaled deeply and turned to her son. "Yes?"

"Grandma Black let the cat out of the bag!"

"I don't think Grandma Black was talking about Sorghum, Cole," Shane quickly corrected.

"This story just keeps getting better." Julianna looked back at him with her teeth set together. "Don't make me regret this, Shane. You need to get your mom to fall in line. We agreed that I'd decide when the time is right."

"I know." He hated the situation.

"Come on, Cole." Julianna turned to walk up the hill.

"No, Mama. Please, I caught a bass as big as me. I want to show it to Grandma Black." Cole attempted to hoist the giant fish out of the five-gallon bucket to display for his mother, but it quickly flipped out of his grasp and fell back into the container "Can't we please eat at the big house tonight?"

"Not tonight, son. Mama needs a break from the Blacks. She's had about all she can take of that family for one day."

Cole's visage betrayed his horrible state of disappointment. He abandoned his pole and his marvelous catch of fish and marched with slumped shoulders toward his mother.

The serrated blade of regret cut Shane through the heart and shredded down through his stomach. He turned away, afraid that he'd lose control of his emotions in front of the boy. Once he felt confident that he'd regained his composure, he looked up at Julianna with a pleading gaze.

She shook her head. "Don't make me out to be the bad guy here. This isn't my fault."

For Cole's sake, Shane replied, "I know. But it's not his fault either. And it's not my parents' fault. Please don't punish them."

Julianna swallowed hard and looked at her son with compassion. "Bring him straight home after supper."

Shane's gaze turned to one of gratitude. "Thank you."

"I can eat at the big house?" Cole seemed unsure, as if his elation might be unwarranted.

"Yes." She knelt beside her son and hugged him. Her eyes flicked to Sorghum who was inspecting the contents of the big orange bucket with the utmost fascination. She then shot Shane one final glare. "And make sure the cats all remain in their respective containment implements."

"I'll do my best." Shane collected the poles and the bucket. "Come on, fellas. Let's get these fish cleaned up for dinner."

Pastor Joel met the anglers at the hydrant where a wide section of an old hickory stump served as the prep table where fish were beheaded and gutted. "Looks like they were biting good today."

Scott Ensley looked up. "This isn't even all of them. Shane made us throw back the little ones."

"Well, them little ones are all bones anyhow." The pastor waved his hand dismissively. "Best wait for them to get big. Then they'll be worth skinning."

Shane smiled at the supportive statement. "I'm going to pour the guts and heads along the garden furrow where we're going to plant the corn. Should make good fertilizer."

The pastor nodded his approval. "Waste not, want not."

"Won't the corn taste like fish?" asked Cole.

"Hopefully not. But if it does, we'll have Grandma Black make it into hush puppies to eat with some catfish," Shane kidded.

The pastor looked at him peculiarly over Tonya Black's new title. "Grandma Black?"

Shane shook his head. "I'll tell you later."

The lot of them walked with Shane as he carried the gut pile down to the garden, the two boys running ahead and leaving Shane and the pastor alone to talk.

Shane thought about the pastor and his brother being young like Scott and Cole. "How did you and the mayor turn out to be so different?"

"Whoooouf!" The pastor's brow creased heavily. "That's a whopper of a question."

"You don't have to answer. I don't mean to pry," said Shane.

"No, that's okay. It just came up out of the blue, that's all." The man seemed to be formulating his response as if still trying to make sense of it all. "Our old man," Pastor Joel paused. "Our father was a harsh man. Violent. He was the type of man who ruled with absolute authority, the kind who didn't need a reason to be angry, but always seemed to find one. He also held his own particular set of standards; standards that the rest of my family could never hope to attain. When we fell short, our failures were met with a belt, a backhand slap, or sometimes a closed fist.

"All of us had our own way of dealing with dear old Dad. Mother tried to stay below the radar. I pushed back. Rebellion was my outlet. Figured if I was going to get kicked around like a dog, I might as well do something to earn it.

"But not Wallace. He tried to please dad. He was in denial. He thought if he just worked hard enough, achieved enough, earned enough money, he'd show Dad that he was worthy of his approval. That never happened. My dad went to his grave telling all of us how worthless we were.

"That hasn't stopped Wallace. I'm convinced his out-of-proportion political ambitions and his unhealthy drive to be financially successful, regardless of what laws have to be bent or broken, all stem from some deep-seated need to please a dead man who couldn't even be satisfied when he was alive.

"I've tried to talk to him about it, but he'll have none of it."

The pastor was quiet for a while, then said with a faint smile, "I spent the better part of my prison sentence performing a post-mortem on my childhood. Took me a long time to make peace with it. Couldn't nobody but Jesus haul me out of that mud hole. But I've forgiven the man and learned that I have to take responsibility for my own actions.

"No judge or jury in this world nor the next will give you a pass for your bad behavior based on having a hard time as a kid." The pastor shook his head. "I wish I could get him to see the light; both for his sake and for his family's."

"He has kids?"

"One. Evelyn, she's twelve. She has cerebral palsy. Smart as a whip. She uses crutches to get around. Speaks relatively clearly. But I haven't seen her in two years. Wallace won't let me visit. The only time I've ever gotten to meet her was when I'd see her at the grocery store or around town with her mother.

"I suspect Wallace wants to make sure he has a

nice stack of money to provide for her care after he's gone. But the way he's doing it is jeopardizing her future more than he knows. Of course, his money is as worthless as everybody else's these days.

"That won't stop him from trying to get a piece of the pie. I'm sure he's thinking of Evelyn, but the ends do not justify the means.

"He's certainly a better father than the example he had. Loves that girl to pieces. He's a better father than he is a man. But like I said, no one gets a pass based on how they were treated. We're all responsible for our own sin."

Shane emptied the fish guts out of the bucket, spreading them evenly down the furrow. "Cole, you want to take the bucket down to the creek and rinse it out?"

"Sure." Cole retrieved the big orange container and set out on his mission with Scott beside him.

Shane kicked clods of dirt over the guts. "Despite all the water that's been under the bridge, Mayor Hayes is still your brother. Do you think it will be hard to have an active role in his abduction?"

"Most of the time, doing the right thing is hard." Pastor Joel looked Shane in the eyes. "The only thing harder than doing the right thing is living with the regret for doing the wrong thing." The pastor turned to watch Cole coming up the hill with the rinsed bucket. "But I suspect I'm preaching to the choir, talking to you about all of that."

Shane had not told the pastor about the situation with Julianna and Cole. He guessed that the man had figured it out for himself. Shane ignored the comment. "We should get these fillets up to the house."

"Sounds like a plan." Pastor Joel patted Shane on the back. "Remember, dwelling on the past won't do you any good. The best course of action is to focus on the present and build a solid foundation for the future. You can't change the past but you can make the most out of today."

"Thanks." That was exactly what Shane needed to hear.

CHAPTER 3

This civilization is rapidly passing away, however. Let us rejoice or else lament the fact as much as every one of us likes; but do not let us shut our eyes to it.

Joseph Schumpeter

Friday afternoon, Shane and Bobby drove into town. Shane scanned through the stations. "Looks like they're all off the air except NPR."

"Who'd have thought the last station standing would be the one that never made a dime?"

Shane lifted his shoulders and turned up the volume.

A male reporter said, "Despite pressure from the

IMF, the global community at large is continuing to reject America's new gold dollar for trade. Other international currencies are showing signs of weakness as they lose value against actual gold, which is quickly becoming the preferred form of trade settlement for oil.

"China, Russia, and the EU have all proposed to let their respective currencies step in as the world reserve currency for the failed US dollar. Likewise, the IMF recommended a block-chain-based version of the SDR to serve as the global standard.

"However, it has been the leaders of OPEC who have set the pace for global trade. The Secretary General of OPEC has stated previously that the cartel is vastly underrepresented by the basket of currencies which make up the SDR. Additionally, he has said that it would not be in the best interest of OPEC's member nations to use the RMB, ruble, or euro for global trade settlement as it would only serve to artificially prop up the value of the chosen currency. Consequently, such an artificial strengthening of a currency would allow the issuing country to abuse their monetary system in much the same way as the US has in the past.

"It is this official stance of the oil cartel and their preference for gold settlement which has re-established the yellow metal as the de-facto reserve currency. Once considered only an archaic relic by investors, gold has nearly doubled against global currencies since the collapse of the US dollar.

"Here at home, currency is local. States along the northern border are using Canadian dollars when they can get a hold of them. Likewise, southwestern states are adopting the peso. In the heartland, barter exchanges and even locally issued scrip are taking the place of the failed dollar.

"Barter exchanges and local currencies matter little to the 90 percent of Americans living in major population centers where resources are scarce and the threat of violence hangs overhead like a storm cloud.

"The UN is working with FEMA to provide basic necessities in the largest cities of the US, but the effort has been fraught with misfortune. Logistical delays, missing trucks filled with supplies, workers abandoning their posts, and well-structured gangs hijacking delivery convoys have left the residents of many US cities perilously close to starvation.

"Rolling blackouts have compounded the crisis in many cities as several major power companies have gone offline while waiting for the federal government to step in and nationalize utilities. Other cities have endured water shortages due to the government's slow response in taking over treatment facilities and pump stations.

"In a statement early this morning from the White House Press Secretary, the Donovan administration said that help is on the way for our domestic complications. The US military is wrapping up the final recall of US troops stationed abroad. These soldiers will be tasked with fulfilling civic roles here at home. However, the DOD has said that more than eighty-five percent of all troops will have to be furloughed indefinitely due to budgetary restraints.

"Those troops who keep their employment will be retrained and repurposed to provide security in the most-troubled cities in the country as well as work in the newly-nationalized utilities sector. With the financial failure of the nation's water, communications, and power companies, these troops will be working to provide the country's most basic infrastructure needs.

"The Donovan administration has submitted a request for another round of aid from the UN, World Bank, and IMF, but delegates from those organizations are asking the US to take on more austerity measures by cutting all non-essential government programs and to consider digging even deeper by selling off US military assets.

"Previous auctions of weapons, planes, and ships have been restricted to US allies, but the UN has urged the US to seek better prices by opening up the auctions to all countries who do not have active United Nations sanctions against them.

"Furthermore, the Pentagon will continue to act as a middleman between foreign buyers and US-based defense contractors such as Northrop Grumman, Lockheed Martin, and Boeing. This will allow the federal government to maintain a minimal income stream since tax revenues are completely non-existent until a standardized currency can replace the dollar."

"We might not be able to manage our finances very well, but we can still build a good bomb," Shane laughed.

Bobby grinned. "Gotta *boom* where you're

planted."

Shane rolled his eyes at the corny joke and drove down Main Street. "Everything is closed up. Looks like a ghost town."

Bobby seemed unaccustomed to small-town life. "I can't imagine it ever being a bustling hub of activity."

"It never looked like Nashville, but Main Street used to be hopping." Shane turned down Municipal Drive and parked at the Sylva Municipal Hall. He got out and led the way to the door. Shane tugged at the handle, but it was locked.

"Nobody home?" asked Bobby.

Shane shielded the glare of the glass door with his hand and looked inside. "Lights are on." He knocked.

A tall lanky police officer with sunken eyes, gray skin, and sharp cheekbones came to the door. "Do you have an appointment?" he asked through the glass.

"I'm Shane Black. I wanted to speak with the mayor."

"Wait here." The man left them standing outside the door.

Bobby chuckled.

"What's funny?" asked Shane.

"Lurch."

"Oh, from the Addams Family. Yeah, does kinda resemble him." Shane smiled.

Bobby kept giggling, then finally did an impersonation. "You rang?" He laughed some more.

"I need a straight face for this," Shane

admonished while fighting a contagious smile. "I'm sure people have come up with some nicknames for you over the years."

"Don't even start." Bobby lost his sense of humor suddenly.

"Oh, I hit a nerve. Come on, what was it?"

Bobby simply shook his head. "Nope. Not telling."

Lurch finally returned and unlocked the door. "Five minutes."

"Probably won't even be that long." Shane stepped through the door. "Thanks."

Lurch escorted Shane and Bobby to the mayor's office.

Hayes glanced up as if preoccupied with more pressing matters. "Thank you, Officer Hicks. I'll call if I need you." After the officer had left, Mayor Hayes said, "Shane Black. What an honor to have you in my office. To what do I owe the pleasure?"

"May I have a seat?" Shane asked.

"Please." The mayor motioned with his hand toward the chairs on the other side of his grand mahogany desk.

Shane introduced his companion. "Mr. Mayor, this is Bobby. He was Backwoods' head of security."

The mayor shook his hand. "Pleasure to meet you, Bobby."

Shane and Bobby were seated. "This business with the tax."

"Let me stop you right there." The mayor held up his hand. "Your assessment was levied by the county. I have no say in their matters."

"Officially, I know. But I'm sure you have some influence. I'm coming to you as a friend. We both know my father can be a little cantankerous. Part of the reason I'm here is to apologize if he offended you. Secondly, I wanted to see if there's anything you could do to get me a second chance at filling out a census form. I'd take care of everything. He wouldn't even be involved."

The mayor seemed pleased to have a celebrity in his office begging for a favor. "I've always liked you, Shane. Big fan of Backwoods, too. Sometimes people don't know what's best for them, and those of us who do have to take action for them, even if they don't like it. I respect you coming in here today." The mayor looked inside his desk and retrieved a census form.

Shane took the form and looked it over. "We'll be growing crops and producing something of value. I'm sure we can work out a payment plan that will be in everyone's best interest. My dad doesn't even have to know. It's not like he asks for my permission when he gets his mind made up to do something."

"Oh? Like what?" inquired the heavy-set politician.

"My wedding for one thing."

"You're getting married. I understood that your fiancé had passed away."

"Lilith? She did. But I think she would want me to move on. That's what I would have wanted for her."

"Who is the lucky gal?"

"I'm the lucky one," Shane smiled. "But it's

Julianna Stanley."

"The little red-headed girl. Didn't you and she used to be an item?"

"We did. I guess the close proximity and being there to comfort one another in our time of loss sort of rekindled an old flame." Shane hated this bit of his performance. Nothing needed rekindling on his end, yet Julianna seemed a hopeless case.

"Well that's real nice. Back to what you were saying about your father. What has he gone and done now?"

"Since it is so soon after Will Stanley's passing, and Lilith's for that matter, we wanted to keep it small and discreet. My dad has invited the whole county, making a big to-do about it."

"Not the whole county," the mayor corrected. "I haven't been invited."

"Well consider yourself invited. You'll be my personal guest. It's next Saturday at 11:00 AM."

"Won't your father mind my being there?"

"It's my wedding. I can at least invite the people I want."

The mayor seemed gratified by the opportunity to show up Paul Black. "I'll do my best to attend, Shane. I'm honored that you think so highly of me to extend this most gracious invitation."

"It will be my honor to have you." Shane folded the form and stood up.

The mayor shook his hand. "Have a wonderful weekend. I hope to see you soon. And about working out a payment plan with the county commissioners, I can talk to them for you. I'm sure they'll work out a reasonable solution."

The mayor escorted them out. "Bobby, if you need a job, we've got some openings on the police force which need filling. I think you'd be a good fit."

"Thank you for the offer. I'll think it over." The big man waved on his way out the door.

Officer Hicks locked the door behind them. His grim expression had not changed.

Once inside the truck, Shane said, "That went about as good as can be expected."

"Yeah, but ol' Lurch wasn't fooled by your charade, not for a minute," Bobby chuckled.

"He's a tough nut to crack, that Lurch." Shane pulled out of the parking lot and returned home.

CHAPTER 4

Real patriotism is a willingness to challenge the government when it's wrong.

Ron Paul

One week later.

Late Saturday morning, Shane knocked on Julianna's door. He stood with his arms behind his back waiting.

She answered, leaving the screen door to the trailer closed between them. She looked him over from head to toe, as if examining his sleek black suit, his full black hair, and his chiseled facial features for a flaw. Then, as if finding none, she looked him in the eyes. "What do you want?"

Shane glanced at his watch, then looked Julianna

over, trying to disguise his longing. "It's a quarter till eleven and the mayor still hasn't shown up. We might need you to put on a dress, just in case."

"And what? Walk down the aisle with you?" Her forehead wrinkled and her skin reddened. "I don't think so. I was very clear about my involvement in this cockamamie scheme. I told your dad that I really couldn't stop him if he wanted to defame my name by including it in this befuddled contrivance, but that's where my role ends!"

Shane lowered his gaze. "Please, Julianna. We need this to work. Hayes is planning to use the crisis to reinstitute feudalism and turn us all into serfs, with himself as lord over Jackson County."

She opened the screen door and stepped out onto the grass. "How does that affect me? I'm just a lowly tenant trying to scrape out a living while living at Black Manor, my charming prince." She feigned a curtsy.

"Even if that's really how you feel about us, I can promise you that what we do here today will have tectonic implications on Cole's future."

The corners of her mouth puffed, as if defeated but unwilling to admit it. "What am I supposed to do with Cole? I absolutely won't stand for him being made to witness this crass bit of theatre. He's confused enough as it is."

"I can take him to the big cabin. My mom and Mrs. Farris are making lunch."

"Hanging out with Grandma Black—that should help with the confusion. What's the mayor going to think when the mother of the groom isn't present?"

"He'll expect someone has to be in charge of the

catering. Times being what they are, folks would have to take care of that themselves."

She huffed but then called inside the trailer. "Cole, do you want to go see Mrs. Black at the big cabin?"

He came running to the door. "Grandma Black!"

Annoyance seethed from her eyes and lips. "How can I be expected to get into costume on such short notice?"

He wanted so badly to tell her that he'd marry her right then and there in her dusty overalls and frumpy hair. "People expect…" He searched for a better word but found none. "…the bride to take a little extra time getting ready. I brought you these." He presented a bouquet of daffodils collected from the mailbox at the bottom of the hill.

Her face softened as she looked at the dazzling collection of yellow and white flowers. She took them, looked as if she wanted to thank him, but did not. Instead, she turned away quickly and ascended the steps to the trailer. "I'll get to the stage as quickly as I can."

***

Shane dropped Cole off with his mother, then hurried down to the meadow where seats had been set up in rows between the pond and the garden.

"Can I do anything to help?" asked Shane's sister, Angela.

"See if Julianna needs anything. She's rushing to get ready."

"Sure." Angela hurried off.

A small podium was placed between two sprawling chestnut trees. Shane looked over the crowd in attendance. The Teague clan took up more seats than anyone else. They lived just up the road from the Blacks.

James Teague had been on that mountain since he was a boy. He and his wife Betty served as patriarch and matriarch over the huge family farm which had five separate dwellings and four generations of Teagues living in the immediate proximity of one another.

Next to them were George and Carroll Franz, the goat farmers at the end of the road. Several other neighbors were in attendance, all fully aware of the true purpose of the mock ceremony.

Shane heard tires rolling over crackling gravel and looked up to see a Sylva PD patrol car.

Angela's husband, Greg, pulled his suit jacket over his holster and buttoned the top button. "Is that him?"

"I hope so. If not, this was all for nothing." Shane watched the patrol car park behind the others.

Greg pressed his lips together. "You guys better know what you're doing. Taking on a corrupt system may sound noble and all, but if you can't win, perhaps you'd be better off biting the bullet on this one."

"We'll win," said Shane. "But even if we don't, we can't start compromising. It will never end."

"Some folks might rather live than be buried with their patriotic piety perfectly intact," Greg replied.

"Good ol' Lurch," Bobby commented when

Officer Hicks stepped out of the driver's side.

The lanky gray man walked to the back door and opened it for the mayor.

"I'll walk him down, then you can escort him to his seat, Dan." Shane marched up the hill toward the patrol car.

The mayor shook hands with Shane. "I had some last-minute business to attend to. I hope you didn't hold things up on my account."

"Julianna is still getting ready."

The mayor nodded. "They like to fuss over themselves, don't they?"

"Yes, sir." Shane gave a sincere look. "I'm glad you could make it."

"I wouldn't miss it for the world, even if it's not a real wedding."

Shane's heart stopped. How had the mayor found out? Who had tipped him off? His mouth went dry. He looked at the surrounding trees, searching for teams of snipers lying in wait to cut them all down if they gave anything other than a complete and immediate surrender. With his pale face, he turned to the mayor. "Why would you say that?"

"You've got my derelict brother presiding over the ceremony, I assume. He's no more of a minister than any other jailhouse preacher." The mayor cackled like a hyena over his own sour humor.

Shane forced himself to breathe, trying not to do anything stupid that would show his nervousness.

The mayor slapped Shane on the back. "I'm just foolin' with you. Don't take it so seriously."

Shane forced a grin. "No problem. I guess I'm a little jumpy because of the wedding."

"That's normal, but Julianna, she's a pretty one. You've done well for yourself."

"Thank you." He wished she truly was his.

Dan escorted the mayor and Officer Hicks to their seats near the front in the center of the row. Shane stood in front of the podium, next to Bobby, who was posing as his best man. Pastor Joel stood behind the podium.

Shane looked up the hill to see Julianna and his sister walking down. Julianna wore a simple yellow sundress which matched the daffodils in her hand and accentuated her flowing red hair. His heart jumped, and for a moment, he forgot the true reason for the gathering.

Paul Black seized upon the opportunity as Mayor Hayes and Officer Hicks turned to behold Julianna's stunning beauty. "Mayor, you're under citizen's arrest."

No less than thirty pistols appeared from inside coats and behind backs. Pastor Joel drew an AR-15 from behind the podium.

The mayor looked around. "That's preposterous."

"Every person here has vowed to put a bullet in you if you resist. This is very real." Paul took the sidearm from Lurch.

"Okay." The mayor held up his hands. "On what grounds?"

"You're the architect of this onerous tax which is little more than an illegal land grab. You and your cohorts have come up with this arbitrary assessment with no consultation whatsoever from the public. We're here to remind you that We the People are still in charge. Folks in this country have never been very fond of taxation without representation. You and the county commissioners have betrayed the trust placed in you by the public. We're taking it back."

"I don't know what you have planned, Paul, but this won't end well for you." The mayor stood up reluctantly as Johnny Teague grabbed him by one arm and Fulton Farris held him by the other.

Paul revealed his long-term strategy to the corrupt politician. "You'll be detained until we can hold new elections. If the federal government is able to get back on their feet, we'll turn you over to the FBI. If not, our newly elected county judges, ones not tainted by your Jackson Political Action Committee, will determine your sentence. But today marks the end of your Jack PAC government.

The mayor smirked. "You're sadly mistaken if you think Jack PAC ends with me."

"I have no illusions about how deep the tentacles of this corruption runs, but I'm betting that if we take you out of the way, the rest of them will run like cockroaches looking for a dark corner to hide in." Paul holstered his pistol.

"Where are you taking us?" asked Officer Hicks as he was escorted toward the car by Greg and Dan.

Shane said, "Mr. and Mrs. Franz have a nice old trailer where they store goat feed and other stuff on the addition they bought a few years back. We'll move you to the jail once we have a new sheriff."

"I'm most disappointed in you, Shane," the mayor replied. "To think you would take advantage of our friendship like this."

"The feeling is mutual, Mr. Mayor. And we were never friends." Shane turned his attention back to Julianna. She sighed, turned around to go back to her trailer, and let the flowers fall to the side. She almost looked disappointed that the show was over. Despite all her vehement protests, Shane felt as if he'd somehow let her down again.

Paul addressed the crowd. "We've got food up at the main cabin for everyone. I appreciate you all coming out to support us today, but this isn't over yet. We've got a long way to go, and lots of planning to do."

Paul walked over to his son while the others began meandering toward the main house at the top of the hill. "Julianna is going to have to move into the house. The sheriff will be looking for Hayes as soon as he doesn't come home. This will be his first stop. We have to keep up appearances until the transition is complete."

Shane shook his head. "You have to tell her. She'll knock my head off if I spring this on her."

"Alright." Paul let out a sigh of exasperation. "Let's get this over with."

The two of them walked to the upper clearing and knocked on Julianna's door. She answered. "The mayor and Officer Hicks are gone?"

"Yes. We appreciate your help, but we need you to stay in character for just a little while longer." Paul continued to explain the predicament. "I understand how difficult this must be for you but…"

She cut him off. "No, Paul. You don't have the slightest inkling how hard my life is right now. And you couldn't possibly fathom how horrible this makes me feel. But I suppose I've sold my soul to the devil, or at least to the Blacks, and now I'm cursed to a life beholden to your whims."

Shane pleaded with her. "You can have Bobby's room downstairs. He'll live in the trailer. Then once this is over, you and Cole can stay in the house. You'll have running water. It'll be safer for Cole. I'll move to the trailer with Bobby."

She gazed at the two of them. "I'm like a fly caught in a spider's web. The more I fight, the deeper I become entangled." She focused on Paul. "As long as we're pretending, can we play like I'm still in control of my child's life?"

"Sure, whatever you need." Paul seemed confused. "Just tell me what I can do to help."

"For starters, please don't have Cole start calling you Grandpa." She slammed the door.

CHAPTER 5

Fascism is the stage reached after communism has proved an illusion.

Friedrich Hayek

Shane picked up the walkie-talkie during Pastor Joel's message Sunday morning. It was the voice of Fulton Farris who was on guard duty with Greg at the main gate. "Sheriff's car just turned into the drive."

Paul turned to Shane. "Go see what he wants. Hayes left with Officer Hicks after the ceremony yesterday. Don't offer any information other than that."

"Okay." Shane stepped away from his seat to walk up to the gate.

When he arrived, Sheriff Harvey Hammer and

Deputy Eric Bivens were already out of the car. "Good morning, Sheriff."

"Shane, how are you?"

"Good. How can I help you?"

"Mayor Hayes hasn't been seen since yesterday. This is his last known location."

Shane looked concerned. "That's awful. He left here right after the ceremony. Didn't say where he was going next."

The sheriff stared at Shane, as if studying him to see if he were lying. "I'd love to take you at your word, but I need to have a look around."

"If you have a warrant, that won't be a problem at all," Shane replied politely.

"I was hoping we could avoid all that formality and unpleasantness. The Blacks have always been fine citizens of the county. I was expecting your cooperation, unless you have something to hide."

"Being searched is one level below being accused, Sheriff. We've already entered into the unpleasantness. The formality part isn't an inconvenience whatsoever, at least not to me. And once you produce the warrant, you can absolutely count on my cooperation."

The sheriff's expression soured. "If you make things hard on me, you can bet I'll repay the favor."

"I'd expect nothing less." Shane stood at the gate between Greg and Fulton.

The sheriff turned to get back in his patrol car. "Deputy Bivens will be staying at the gate. He'll search any vehicle coming or going based on probable cause. Eric, I'll send you some backup. If these hillbillies give you any trouble, you're authorized to shoot."

"Yes, sir," said Bivens.

Shane watched the sheriff drive away.

Bivens shook his head. "I hope you haven't done what I think you did. I didn't say anything to Harvey about Pastor Joel's Caesar-and-the-Ides-of-March comment. If I had, you better believe he'd have rolled in hot."

Shane looked across the gate. "Eric, you need to worry about your own involvement. You're propping up a criminal organization, not much different than the mob."

"Nothing like the mob," said Eric. "These are elected officials."

"Acting completely outside of their authority," Shane countered.

"Desperate times." Eric looked at Fulton who said nothing. "You should all be glad you live in a county that still has any form of government at all. I was listening to the radio on the way over and the military is pulling out of Houston. Gangs have taken control. The government is still in charge of Atlanta, but they're on 22-hour lockdown. LA has fallen. Detroit is long gone. Chicago is hanging on by a thread. Even New York has a dusk-to-dawn curfew. We're doing the best we can."

Shane shook his head. "If you're not doing the will of the people, you're a tyrant, pushing your own agenda by force. Be honest with yourself, Eric. You know better."

"I'm trying to hold back the tide. Affect change from inside. Most of the good guys at the sheriff's department and the Sylva PD are gone. The people they are replacing them with are..." He shook his head. "Let's just say they're lowering the bar and taking what they can get. If I leave, trust me, you won't like my replacement."

Shane considered Bivens reasoning. "I appreciate your service, but if you're enabling bad guys, that makes you a bad guy. If you'll excuse me, I've gotta go tell my dad what is going on."

Fulton followed Shane down the drive. His voice sounded scared. "What are we going to do? We can't take on the sheriff's department!"

"Calm down. No one is taking on anyone. The sheriff will go get a warrant. He'll have a look around, find nothing, and leave. What are you worried about?"

"I don't know. What if he comes across a tire track or a hair?"

Shane paused. "So, what if he does? We're not denying that the mayor was here. But he's not now, and that's the truth."

"It's not the whole truth."

"As far as you're concerned, it's enough of the truth. Just go back to the gate and act natural."

Fulton spun around. "Naturally paranoid."

Shane ignored him and sprinted back to the gathering. "Dad, Fulton is spooked. You need to get him off the gate. Replace him with someone else."

Paul nodded. "Dan, can you cover the gate?"

"Sure."

"Thank you. Bobby, you, too. Relieve Greg. Then it just looks like a shift change rather than us trying to sweep one individual under the rug."

"You got it." Bobby grabbed a rifle and walked

up the hill with Dan.

An hour later, Sheriff Hammer arrived with his warrant. He stopped by the gathering area near the pond and shoved a copy into Paul's chest. "Here's your warrant." Hammer looked at the six deputies with him. "Search every room, every corner, attic spaces, cellars, anywhere big enough to put a body or a body part." He glared at Shane. "And don't worry about making a mess of things. We don't owe these people any favors."

"Warrants come fast when the judge owns stock in Jackson Construction." Paul studied the warrant signed by Judge Lidke.

"Warrants come quick when a public official goes missing and the residents of his last known location start acting cagey," Hammer countered.

"What percent interest do you have in Jackson Construction?" Paul inquired.

"Zero," Hammer replied.

"You don't have an S-Corp which is part owner in Jackson Construction?"

"I'm the one asking questions here," Hammer raised his voice. "I don't answer to you."

"Not to me personally, but the residents of Jackson County have turned a blind eye to lots of conflicts of interest and shady deals for a long time. This latest illegal assessment crosses the line. Everyone involved in it will be turned out of office soon enough."

The sheriff crossed his arms. "You're not helping your case here, Paul. Are you sure you want to keep talking?"

"I've said enough." Paul turned his back to the sheriff and waved for Shane to follow him. "Come on, son. Let's go make sure these ruffians aren't busting up the place."

Shane walked beside his father up the steep hill to the main house. "Did you recognize any of those deputies that came in with Hammer?"

"One of them. That Van Burren boy, Jacob, I think. He's one of the town troublemakers. He's been arrested several times. Fighting, drunk and disorderly, stuff like that. His name comes up in the paper about once a year."

Shane nodded. "Bivens said the department is taking anyone they can get."

"That's a bad sign." Paul continued marching up the hill.

***

The sheriff's men spent three hours dumping drawers onto the floor, breaking dishes, and flipping mattresses. Shane and the others were powerless to do anything but stand by and watch. Finally, they came up with no evidence linking any of the residents of the Blacks' compound to a crime. Sheriff Hammer looked angry, as if he'd missed something. "Paul, Shane, don't get too comfortable. I may be back. Either way, we'll be watching. I'm leaving Eric Bivens outside the gate. You'll slip up. And when you do, I'll be there." The sheriff waved his hands. "Come on boys. Let's get out of here."

Once the sheriff and his men had left, Paul called everyone together by the fire pit. "We need to move fast to hold the snap election."

"Hammer, Judge Lidke, the county commissioners, they'll never recognize the snap election as being legitimate." Greg sat on the ground with his back against a tree.

"Doesn't matter. The people will recognize it. This tax has pushed the citizens of Jackson County over the edge. They're fighting mad," said Paul.

Fulton Ferris looked nervously from one person to the next. "Sheriff Hammer seems not to care what the citizens think. I believe they've decided to no longer take popular opinion into consideration when they declared the tax."

"You may be right about that, Fulton. But I think I speak for most everyone here when I say we're not concerning ourselves with the city and county officials' feelings." Pastor Joel crossed his arms.

Fulton's voice went high and he held his palm out. "What are we going to do? Start a war with the Sylva PD and Jackson County Sheriff's Department?"

"No." Paul let his hand rest on the handle of his pistol at his side. "We have no quarrel with the departments. But if the administrators refuse to accept the will of the people and we have to unseat them by force, so be it."

Fulton bit his fingernail and looked at his wife, Maggie, with worried eyes.

"I'm with Dad." Angela put her arm around Greg. "I don't want to be pushed around any longer."

"I think everyone knows I'm done with being taken advantage of by people looking to profit off of the crisis." Julianna sat in one of the Adirondack chairs with Cole sitting in her lap.

"Amen to that!" Mrs. Perkins said. "I'll run for commissioner if there ain't no age limit. I might not know much about governin', but I ain't out to swindle nobody."

"Thank you, Mrs. Perkins. We'll put your name in the hat." Paul looked at the man beside him. "Pastor Joel is running for mayor. We need another candidate since the incumbent is— indisposed."

"Why don't you run, dad?" Shane asked.

"Thank you for your support, son. But I'll be running against Harvey Hammer. Besides, it should be someone who doesn't live at the compound."

"I nominate Jimmy Teague," said Dan.

"Good suggestion. I'll run by there after we break and see if he'd be interested. Not many folks want anything to do with governing right now. It's all they can do to keep food on the table. If Pastor Joel and I serve, the rest of you will have to pick up our slack. This has to be a unanimous decision."

Kari Ensley sat in another of the chairs with Scott in her lap. "We were going to be slaving away to pay Mayor Hayes' tax anyway. I'd rather pull some extra shifts so you and Pastor Joel can provide an honest government." She looked around at the others. "Does everyone agree?"

Shane began clapping in support of the statement. Elizabeth Hayes joined him. Soon, everyone except Fulton and Maggie Farris was applauding.

CHAPTER 6

All things have I seen in the days of my vanity: there is a just man that perisheth in his righteousness, and there is a wicked man that prolongeth his life in his wickedness.

Ecclesiastes 7:15

Ten days later.

Shane finished breakfast Tuesday morning before daylight.

Tonya snapped the lid on a plastic food container. "Here's the mayor's and Officer Hicks' food. Can you run it over to the trailer at the Franzs' property?"

Shane inspected the contents. "You're giving

them eggs and pancakes?"

Tonya rinsed her hands under the sink. "It's probably the last good meal they'll get. After the election today, I'm sure they'll be transferred to the county jail to await trial. I can't imagine the gruel they'll be fed there."

Shane liked his mother's graciousness when it was toward him, but didn't like to see it so freely provided to the likes of Wallace Hayes and Lurch. He wrinkled his brow but made no other objections. "I'll be back."

Shane strapped on his gun belt and headed into the woods. The trail to the Franzs' property through the forest was well worn. Thanks to having a deputy posted outside the Blacks' gate, all food runs to bring the mayor's and Hicks' meals had to utilize the back way. Shane kept his flashlight low and rolled his feet to minimize the sound of leaves crunching beneath his feet.

He whispered to himself to keep his mind occupied on the prolonged hike. "At least the surreptitious segment of this operation will be drawing to a close today. I feel bad for Hayes' daughter, not knowing where her father is. But when she discovers that he's a self-imposed dictator guilty of the worst kind of corruption and embezzlement, she may wish she'd never found out. I guess ignorance really is bliss, but at least she'll have closure this way."

Shane saw the trailer in the middle of the goat pasture from inside the tree line. He considered feeding one of the breakfasts to the goats and leaving the other for the two criminals to share. His mother's cooking was far too good for Hayes and Lurch. He emerged from the woods and approached the dilapidated trailer. The first glint of daylight peeked over the mountain in the east. It provided just enough illumination for Shane to see without the aid of his flashlight. "The door is open!" Shane drew his pistol and proceeded inside. "They're gone!" Shane dropped the food containers and sprinted back to the house.

Once back to the main cabin, Shane explained to his father what he'd found.

"Did it look like they'd broken out?" Paul asked.

Pastor Joel inquired, "How could they? We had them cuffed to chains which were fed through holes in the floor and locked to the trailer axle."

"The cuffs and chains were still there." Shane shook his head.

"Could they have picked the cuffs?" Paul stroked his beard.

"I don't think so. Bobby and I searched them twice when we locked them up. We checked the area every time we went to make sure they didn't find anything to use for a pick." Shane glanced at Fulton. "I think someone let them out."

"Why are you looking at me?" Fulton sounded defensive.

"It's no secret that you're not entirely on board with our plan to take back the local government." Shane eyed him with distrust.

"I'm not entirely comfortable with your tactics, but I understand the reasoning behind it. I'd never do anything to undermine your plan." Fulton turned to Paul. "We've known each other for a long time.

You have to believe me."

Paul studied his old friend. "I'd like to, Fulton. But it doesn't look good. Shane, go call the people from the trailers. Pull Bobby and Dan off the gate. That's the least of our worries right now. We need to put a plan together."

Fifteen minutes later everyone was gathered at the main house and all of them were in a tizzy.

Dan Ensley said, "I've got a hunting cabin down *off* Tilley Creek."

"We're sixteen people. Even if we could all squeeze into a hunting cabin, that's a pretty big logistical challenge." Paul looked at the people depending on him for a plan.

"Do you think this guy is going to let us out on bail?" asked Bobby.

"I doubt it," Pastor Joel said grimly.

"Then we shouldn't just sit here and make it easy for him. Let's at least make Hayes work for it if he's going to catch us," Bobby added.

Paul looked at Dan. "Why don't you take the women and children to your cabin?"

"I can do that," Dan answered.

"Tonya, rally your troops. Be out of here in fifteen minutes." Paul clapped his hands. "Come on, ladies, let's move out."

"What will you do?" Tonya asked.

"We'll figure that out as we go." He turned to Shane. "Come on. We've got work to do."

Shane followed his father down the stairs to the basement. "What are we going to do?"

"Stash some guns, ammo, and gold. You can bet your bottom dollar that Hayes and Hammer are

47

putting together an assault team as we speak. They'll use this as an excuse to seize everything we've got of value."

"Shouldn't we run?"

"Where?"

"I don't know, the Teagues' maybe?"

"Hayes might be locking them up also. Anyone we can count on will be a target. Besides, we have to work under the assumption that we have a traitor among us." Paul opened the safe. "Set up the GameSaver. We'll vacuum pack some pistols, rifles, and ammo. We'll haul them up the hill and find a place to bury them."

"By traitor, you mean Fulton." Shane began to carry out his father's instructions.

"We don't know that for sure."

"Johnnie Cochran himself couldn't convince me that Fulton Farris isn't the one behind this." Shane cut lengths of sealing plastic long enough to fit over the rifles.

"Cochran is dead."

"Then Fulton doesn't have a prayer of being acquitted." Shane sealed one side of the plastic sheeting and handed it to his father.

"Innocent until proven guilty." Paul slid the plastic sleeve over the rifle and gave it to Shane.

Shane set the GameSaver and began the vacuum process. "Should I get Bobby to help us?"

"We need to keep this between you and me."

"Bobby didn't set the mayor free. You can take that to the bank."

"Right now, I trust you and I trust me. I'm not ready to bank or bet on anyone else."

"Okay." Shane began sealing the next weapon.

***

Half an hour later, Shane worked feverishly to dig a hole just below the old logging road which ran between the back-property line and main cabin.

Paul pulled the plastic-wrapped weapons out of a long duffle bag. "This is another one of those things I never got around to doing."

"You got around to doing more things than most of us." Shane wiped the sweat off his brow. "Think that will do it?"

"If we had more time, I'd say go deeper. But as it stands, that will be fine." Paul carefully stacked three AR-15s on top of one another.

Shane placed five ammo cans side by side. "Where did you put your gold?"

"It's in the small .30 cal ammo can."

"We didn't vacuum seal it." The gold coins which Shane had bought before coming home were sealed in the thick FoodSaver plastic. They were tucked inside a plastic coffee can along with the diamond ring he'd bought for Lilith. The red plastic container was wrapped tightly with an excessive amount of duct tape. He nestled the messy-looking object next to the metal ammo cans.

"I know," said Paul. "Gold won't tarnish. Still, if we'd had more time, I'd have done it." Paul grabbed the shovel and began covering the cache. Shane used the garden rake to pull leaves and sticks from the forest floor over the dirt.

"Far from perfect, but it will have to do." Paul

began walking back down the trail to the main house. "Let's get back before Hayes and Hammer show up."

Once back to the house, Greg and Pastor Joel were gearing up.

"Where are you headed?" Paul asked.

"Over the hill." Greg tightened the strap on his pack. "We'll follow Soapstone Creek to the ridgeline. From there, we can set up camp in the mountains for a day or two. It will give us time to think."

"It's a good plan, Paul. You should come." Pastor Joel loaded his rifle and slung it over his back.

Paul turned to Shane. "What do you think?"

"I think we're out of time, and it's the best thing going," he replied.

"Can you and Bobby be ready to roll out in ten?" Paul asked.

"I can. Bobby?" Shane turned to his friend.

"I'm already packed." The big man smiled and lifted a pack sitting on the floor near his feet.

"Don't wait for me. I'll catch up." Shane hustled up to his room.

Five minutes later, his father called up the stairs. "We're rolling out now. We'll slow down once we're over the hill. You know the way?"

"Yep. If I'm not up to you by then, I'll see you at the top of Soapstone Creek." Shane rushed to get his pack loaded, wishing it had already been done.

Finally, his preparations were complete. He hoisted the bag onto his back, tucked his pistol in his waistband holster, and shouldered his shotgun.

He looked out the window to see four Jackson County Sheriff's Department patrol cars coming up the drive. His heart raced. Shane bounded down the stairs and out the back door. He leaped up on the short railroad tie retaining wall, sprinted behind the firewood shelter racks and into the woods. Only the smallest leaves were on the trees in early April so he had to get to the ridgeline before the sheriff's men got up to the main house and started looking for him. Otherwise, they'd spot him and he'd tip them off to the direction in which the others were traveling.

His feet found the familiar steps which trekked up, then down below a thicket of holly trees before the trail resumed its upward trend. Shane huffed, gasping for air as he neared the ridge. Once there, he slowed and turned to look if he'd been spotted. He lay prone on the forest floor and watched quietly. If Hammer's men were coming, he'd lead them south, giving his father and the others a chance to get away. Shane listened to the men getting out of their cars.

"Search the house," said one of the deputies. "The sheriff said they've got a nice little stash of supplies. Load up as much as you can."

Shane's blood began to boil as he watched the deputies kick in his door to pillage the cabin. On the bright side, however, the sheriff's men seemed more concerned with the loot than pursuing Shane and his group. Shane slowly backed away from his observation position. He maneuvered through the heavy brush trying to catch up with his father and the others.

His easterly route would eventually run into Posey Blanton Road. From there, he could follow the road to Soapstone Creek. Shane fought against the thorny branches in the undergrowth. He stepped high to keep his ankles from getting tangled in the briars. "Can't be much further," he said to himself.

Finally, he saw Bobby's towering figure in the distance. "There they are." Shane picked up his pace. Soon, he could make out his father, Pastor Joel, and Fulton. He watched as Greg led them out onto the road. Paul turned around, as if looking for Shane. He waved his hand, but his father didn't see him. Shane was tempted to call out to him, but he knew it wouldn't be prudent considering the circumstances. "No matter, I'll catch up to them soon enough."

Shane couldn't wait to tell them that the sheriff's men weren't giving them chase through the woods. Suddenly, he heard the sound of car engines and screeching tires. Next, he heard Sheriff Hammer's voice over a patrol car intercom. "Face down! On the ground!"

Shane watched his father's group freeze in the middle of the road.

"Do it now!" Hammer repeated. "This is your last chance before my men open fire."

Shane racked a shell into his shotgun. He couldn't take on the entire department, but he could kill Fulton Farris. "That dirty rat! He led them straight into a trap! No wonder they didn't follow me into the woods. Fulton must have radioed our plans to Hammer." Shane took aim. But then, he realized, if Fulton had sold out his group, he'd also reported on the general location of the women and children.

If Shane chose to engage with the enemy here, he'd lose. Additionally, it would only be a matter of time before Hammer found Dan's cabin. He listened closely.

Harvey Hammer stood over his captives while deputies placed wrist restraints on each of them. "Where's Shane?"

Hammer kicked Paul in the ribs. "I asked you a question."

Paul said nothing.

Next, Hammer placed his boot on the neck of Fulton. "Where is he?"

Fulton likewise said nothing.

Hammer pressed down on his throat. From his vantage point, Shane could see Fulton's face turning red. Hammer lifted his foot and repeated his question. "I can do this all day. Where is Shane Black?"

"He got a late start," Fulton said between gasps.

Harvey Hammer looked around at his men. "Where's the K-9 unit? Get the dogs into those woods."

Shane knew he'd never evade the dogs unless he got a good head start. He got up from his position and headed south. His only hope was to get far enough away and move through rough enough terrain so as to tire out the dogs and their handlers.

It didn't take long for the dogs to catch his scent. He heard them barking behind him. The sound boosted his adrenal glands, enabling him to move faster. Every time he saw a thicket of holly trees, he bolted in that direction, leading the animals and the deputies through the worst possible path. Sharp leaves pricked his hands and thorny briars growing around the hollies scraped his face. He paid no mind to the minor discomforts and thought only of getting to Dan's hunting cabin in time to warn his mother, to get Julianna and his son out of harm's way.

The barking persisted for more than an hour, but Shane maintained his lead. He felt his muscles growing tired, the energy running out of his core, and his adrenaline dying off. "I've gotta do something. I'm going to give out before the dogs." Shane kept moving, scanning the wilderness for a better opportunity. Finally, he saw a steep incline. Rocks jetting out of the cliff bounded skyward more than twenty-five feet. "That's going to be a hard climb even with opposable thumbs. Sorry, my four-footed friends. This is where our journey together ends." Shane quickly dropped his pack and stowed his shotgun inside. He put the bag on his shoulders once more and tightened the straps as rapidly as he could. Then, he began his race toward the summit. The first fifteen feet was relatively easy. But the last section of the climb had few footholds.

He reached for a sharp knob for support. He needed this grip to get him across the face of the rock where his next step would lead him higher. The knob crumbled when he put his weight on it. Shane lost his balance and slid down the rock.

He clawed at the ledge where he'd been standing and narrowly arrested his downward plummet. His hands shook with fear. Panic threatened to set in. He took a deep breath and waited to regain his composure. The sound of the dogs grew louder. "Live or die, I have to keep going."

Shane summoned all of his strength and reworked his way back to the ledge. With nothing to steady himself, he'd have to leap for the next slender jut of rock. He focused on the four-inch wide shelf, which was six feet away from where he stood. He took a deep breath and readied himself. He hesitated for a moment, but the barks of his pursuers grew nearer. "I have to go. I have to do it now." He clenched his jaw and jumped!

CHAPTER 7

Behold, the eye of the Lord is upon them that fear him, upon them that hope in his mercy; to deliver their soul from death, and to keep them alive in famine. Our soul waiteth for the Lord: he is our help and our shield.

Psalm 33:18-20

Shane landed squarely on the narrow sliver of stone with his hands out like an eagle's claws, each finger searching for the minutest indentation to steady his body against the face of the large monolith. Having accomplished the death-defying feat, Shane refocused and continued his assent. No sooner had he climbed upon the cliff of the giant geological feature than the sound of the dogs and their handlers arrived. Shane lay silent and still just above, not wanting to let them know how close they were to apprehending him. He listened to the voices of the handlers.

"He went up," said one.

"What are we going to do? Follow him?"

The first laughed. "Yeah, be my guest. I don't even know how he pulled it off. Look at that incline. It goes straight up. Even if we could get up there, we'd never be able to get the dogs up. He'd be long gone by the time we scaled that rock. And we'd have no way to track him.

"Call it in. Tell Hammer he's headed southeast."

"What's southeast?" asked the other.

"I don't know. Wolf Creek Lake, Balsam Grove, Lake Toxaway, lots of real-estate, that's what."

Shane continued to listen as the men conversed with the sheriff over the radio. He didn't want to risk making a sound, but he also needed the rest. He didn't dare move a muscle. Soon, the men left with the dogs and Shane slowly resumed his course. He had no map, no compass, and had lost his direction. With the sun being nearly directly overhead, the only clue he had was that the K-9 handlers estimated his general track to be toward the southeast. Shane tacked in the direction that he guessed to be the southwest, both to get off the track on which Hammer was expecting him to move and to aim toward the general direction of Dan's hunting cabin.

Shane hiked for another hour before pausing to address his injuries and get a drink of water. Shane spotted several plantain weeds growing just outside the tree line on his trek. He plucked a few of the distinct leaves growing out from a center crown. He chewed the leaves into a poultice and applied a pinch to each of the reddened scrapes and scratches he'd received by choosing the path less traveled. The swelling and discomfort seemed to subside almost instantly, just as when his father had used the plant on his cuts and stings as a boy.

Shane sipped from his single water bottle, knowing he'd need to locate more soon. In his haste, he'd not taken a water filter and had only two days' worth of food. Shane picked as many of the plantain leaves as he could find, eating some for the abundance of vitamins and minerals and stashing the rest in his side pockets to augment his sparse food stores.

As the afternoon progressed and the sun moved lower, Shane was able to better discern his directions. "If I can hit the Tuskegee River, I should be able to trace the roads to Tilley Creek. Still, finding Dan's cabin will be like looking for a gnat in a briar patch."

Two hours passed, and Shane found a creek. He refilled his water bottle and said a quick prayer for God to keep him from getting sick by drinking it. "The creek is running right in the direction I want to go. It should take me straight to the river." A road also ran alongside the creek. Shane kept away from the pavement and out of sight to anyone driving by.

Shane finally made it to the river late Tuesday afternoon. The next section of his travels would take him through Cullowhee. The area was more populated than he liked, but without a map, it was his only choice. He had to get to Tilley Creek Road. He had to find his mother, Julianna, and Cole before Hammer did.

The sun was low by the time Shane made it to the mountain road. He came out of the woods to examine the street sign. "Presley Creek. Dan said his cabin was off Tilley Creek Road, not on Tilley Creek. I don't know of too many other paved roads off Tilley Creek."

Shane looked up to his Creator. "God, I could use your divine wisdom about now. I'm wandering in the dark here." He looked toward the sun dipping behind the mountain. "Literally wandering in the dark in less than an hour from now. Please, I really need your guidance."

Shane continued up the road staying near the tree line. He'd not seen a vehicle since crossing the river and figured he'd have plenty of time to hide if he heard one coming. An hour later, the sun was gone and clouds were rolling in to obscure the frail bit of light still glowing in the west. "Smells like rain. I have to find a shelter." Seeing a gravel road leading off the pavement, he followed it. He passed two houses which had lights on, walking quietly so as not to alert them or their dogs of his presence. Near the end of the road, Shane saw what looked like an old livestock shelter, for goats most likely. "That looks like my spot for the night."

Cautiously, he crossed the fence and ducked low as he walked through a narrow meadow. He placed his pack on the ground gently. Shane opened his pack, putting on an extra sweatshirt and a pair of sweatpants over his cargo pants. The night air was cooling rapidly. The rain would likely make it even colder. Shane took out one of the MRE's from his pack. He had to rely on his sense of touch in order to eat it in the pitch-black darkness of the rainy night.

The first drops of rain pecked against the metal roof of the shelter. Shane positioned himself with his head elevated against the pack and closed his eyes. The hypnotic sound of the pattering rain combined with his absolute exhaustion soon sucked him into a deep, heavy sleep.

***

"Wake up!"

Shane opened his eyes to a blinding light pointed in his face.

An intimidating voice yelled, "If you go for that gun, I'll blow your head clean off your shoulders, boy!"

Shane shielded his eyes. "I'm sorry, I just needed to rest my eyes for a while. I got lost out here and I don't have a map."

"Shane? Is that you?"

The voice sounded familiar, but he was blinded by the light. "Dan?"

"What are you doing out here in the rain? Come on in the house and get warm."

Shane felt a hand grip his own. His eyes struggled to regain vision. He let Dan help him up off the ground. "Hammer took everyone else. We tried to go over the ridge, but the sheriff was waiting for us. We've got a mole."

"I figured that." Dan picked up Shane's pack and shotgun from the ground.

"We have to get the girls out of here. If Fulton is the mole, he heard you say that you were bringing them to the Tilly Creek area."

"They're not here. I kinda figured we had ourselves a snitch. My great grandfather had a little place way out toward Murphy. The law looked for that place from 1920 until 1933. Never found it. Hammer won't get his hands on them out there."

With his head groggy from just waking up, Shane tried to figure out the significance of the dates Dan had given him. "He ran a still?"

"We don't call it that. All my people are Baptists. Folks used his recipe for cough syrup and home remedies back then. Anyhow, the girls are safe out at Pawpaw's medicine factory."

Shane silently thanked God for leading him to Dan.

Dan opened the creaky door to the simple old dwelling. Shane walked in. A single oil lantern lit the room. Shane looked in the corner to see Deputy Bivens sitting at the rustic old table. Shane instinctively drew his gun. "Dan! You're the mole!"

"Calm down there, Hoss!" Dan held his hands up as did Deputy Bivens.

Shane pointed the pistol from one to the other. "What's he doing here?"

"I called him," Dan said. "After I knew the girls were safe. We needed an ally inside Hammer's camp."

"And you've suddenly decided to flip?" Shane

leveled the pistol at Bivens' head.

"Not suddenly, but yes, I'm on your side." Bivens stood up from the rough wood table. "Will you please stop pointing that thing at me?"

"As soon as I'm convinced," Shane said.

"I had the drop on you out there in the field, Shane!" Dan presented his case. "If we'd have wanted to take you down, we had you trapped like a snake in a bucket."

Shane could not dispute the reasoning and holstered his weapon. "Okay. So you're going to help us?"

Bivens looked perplexed. "I know the mayor and the sheriff are out of control. They've always found ways to profit off their roles in government. It rubs me wrong, but the people put them in office."

"Those votes were bought and paid for by Jack PAC." Shane crossed his arms.

"You can't buy a vote unless it's for sale," Bivens countered. "Still, two wrongs don't make a right. Same goes for you and your dad. I agree that Hayes and Hammer stepped way over the line of what's legal with this special assessment. But that doesn't justify kidnapping."

Shane's brow creased. "He pushed us up against a wall. We had no legal options. Mayor Hayes had to be taken out of the way until we could hold new elections. Otherwise, he'd interfere, buy off just enough people to stay in power, and we'd either bend to his extortion or lose our farm. Neither of those outcomes is acceptable to me nor my father."

Bivens pressed his lips together. "Well, you're about to lose everything anyway. You've successfully jumped out of the frying pan and straight into the fire. Come Thursday morning, the mayor is holding trial for your father, Pastor Joel, and the others."

"So fast?" Shane inquired.

"Yeah, and it gets worse," Bivens added.

"Oh?"

"Judge Lidke will be hearing the case. No jury. Lidke says it would be impossible to find jurors who are impartial to the case in Jackson County. And due to the crisis, moving the trial to another jurisdiction is out of the question."

"I bet it is," Shane snarled. "That would bring all of Jack PAC's sins to light. I suppose Judge Lidke will be sentencing them if they're found guilty?"

"When they're found guilty," Bivens corrected. "Hayes wants this thing wrapped up by Friday afternoon. He plans on hanging the lot of them Saturday morning on the courthouse lawn."

"What? Kidnapping isn't a capital offense! Even if it were, they'd have the right to an appeal." Shane quickly saw the seriousness of the situation.

"I know," said Bivens. "Lidke is running a total kangaroo court. It's what pushed me over the edge. I still disagree with the way your group handled things, but at this point, you're clearly the lesser of the two evils."

His statement didn't quite come off as a compliment, so Shane didn't bother to thank him. "What about the other people who were at the wedding? Were they locked up?"

"No. Hayes has a patrol car sitting on the Teagues' compound and the Franzs', but he's hoping to make an example out of the people from your group. He expects the others will fall in line after the execution."

"We have to bust them out," said Shane. "Before the trial."

"How do you propose to do that?" Bivens asked. "We're three people. We can't take on Hammer."

"We'll get the Teagues. There's enough of them to make a small army," Dan suggested.

"They're being watched around the clock. Even if you could get a message to them, they could never mobilize without drawing suspicion." Eric Bivens shot down the idea before it had a chance to take root as a valid alternative.

"What about some of the other deputies who left because of how bad things have gotten?" asked Shane. "Would any of them help us out?"

"Harris, Thompson, and maybe Sabas." Eric seemed to be thinking of any other possibilities. "But Hammer has brought in so many thugs, we'd be outnumbered two-to-one even if we had every good deputy who'd ever worked at the department."

"Then we need leverage against them," said Dan.

Bivens shook his head. "They don't care about anything but themselves, especially the mayor."

"That might not be entirely true." Shane took a seat at the rickety old table.

"Explain," said Bivens.

"Wallace Hayes has a daughter that's very dear to him."

"Evelyn? She has cerebral palsy. We're not touching her!" Bivens scowled.

"She might be our only option," Shane argued.

"No way. We're not hurting a crippled child." Bivens slammed his fist on the table.

"We're not going to hurt her." Shane held up his hand.

"Then what are you talking about?" Bivens asked.

"The mayor doesn't know that we won't hurt her. We just need to make him think something might happen," said Shane.

"But you'd have to abduct her. That would frighten her to death." Bivens looked at Shane as if he'd gone mad. "Didn't your group just go through that with Julianna and Will's kid?"

Even though he hadn't known Cole was his son at the time, Shane knew exactly what it felt like. "What's better, to scare a little girl for a day or two or sit back and let my father and the others die?"

Bivens shook his head. "You're way too liberal in your application of situational ethics. Nothing can justify what you're considering."

"Then you need to come up with a better idea! I won't watch my father, Pastor Joel, Bobby, and Greg be strung up like a troop of wild west horse thieves," Shane rebutted.

Dan stepped in as the peacemaker. "Let's all just take a breath and consider our options here."

All three of the men were quiet for several minutes. Eric Bivens walked toward the door of the simple cabin. "I'll see if I can work out a plan to break them out of the county jail. I'll meet you here tomorrow evening."

CHAPTER 8

A man's heart deviseth his way: but the Lord directeth his steps.

Proverbs 16:9

Shane latched the door behind Bivens. "Do you think we can trust him?"

"Have you got a choice?" asked Dan.

Shane looked out the window as Bivens got into his personal truck and pulled out of the drive. "I'm not going to sit around and wait for him to get us into a boondoggle with this escape plan. We need to start putting together a contingency right now. Will you help me if it comes down to it?"

Dan looked out the window. "Let's hope Bivens can pull off the jailbreak."

"But if he can't, can I count on you?"

"I won't lift a finger to hurt that youngin." Dan's expression displayed his resolution.

"We won't hurt her, I promise."

"What do you have in mind?" asked Dan.

"The mayor lives in the big white house on Haywood Road, doesn't he?"

"That's his house, but I'd imagine he took his family out to the mountains. He's got a great big compound up north of Addie."

"Do you know where it is?"

"I might. He had me come look at it years back. Wanted us to do some remodeling."

"Did you get the job?"

"Nope. He had in mind that I'd work hourly for Jackson Construction while he wrote the job off as repairs. I wanted no part of his convoluted accounting. Sounded like a good way to get shortchanged."

"Can you remember the layout?"

"I was only in the main part of the house and the master bedroom. He wanted to put shiplap walls with tongue-and-groove ceilings throughout the master bedroom and bath. I can remember what I saw of the place."

"Can you try drawing it out?"

"I'll try." Dan rifled through the drawers until he found an old envelope and a pencil. He proceeded to sketch out the road and basic floor plan of the house, explaining the details to Shane.

As badly as Shane wanted to see his mother, sister, Cole, and especially Julianna, he and Dan decided it would be best not to drive out to Pawpaw Ensley's old distillery. If they were followed,

Hammer and Hayes would most certainly arrest the women also.

The next evening, Deputy Bivens drove up the dirt road to the old cabin where Shane and Dan were staying. Shane opened the door. "Did you come up with a plan?"

Bivens kicked the mud off his boots before entering. "I think so."

"Let's hear it," Dan said anxiously.

Bivens took off his jacket and sat at the wobbly table. "I've got one of the correctional officers from the jail willing to help us out. Deputy Ritter."

"Butterbean?" Dan asked.

Bivens frowned at the moniker. "Ritter has lost some weight."

"How much did he lose?" quizzed Dan.

"Fifteen, twenty pounds," Bivens replied.

"Oh, come on! That boy is every bit of three-hundred pounds," argued Dan. "Twenty pounds doesn't even account for one of his chins."

"Forget about all of that," Shane interrupted. "How is one guard going to matter against Hammer's entire department?"

"Because Butterbean, I mean Deputy Ritter drives the transport van."

Shane waited to hear the rest of the plan. "Okay, this is getting better. Please, continue."

Bivens said, "I'll be driving one of the two patrol cars escorting the prisoner transport van. I'm going to run interference for Ritter and block the other escort while he makes a run for it. He's going to drive the van down to the train depot in Dillsboro where we'll have a second vehicle stashed. The cuffs and shackles will be dummy locked, so the prisoners will already be free when he pulls up. They'll bail out and Butterbean will lead the chase vehicles through the mountains. Hopefully, your father and the others will be able to drive the second van here without being spotted."

"The jail is less than a half-mile from the courthouse. Hammer is going to know as soon as Butterbean turns off course." Dan took off his ball cap and scratched his head. "The sheriff will have the entire department after him."

"I don't think so. Hayes is convinced that you'll try some type of rescue attempt. He has every cop and every deputy looking for you. He thinks this is the perfect trap. He's planning on apprehending Shane and hanging him alongside the others Friday morning at dawn."

Shane scoffed, "Ha! Talk about delusions of grandeur."

"We'll use it to our advantage," said Bivens. "While Hayes is looking left, we'll hit him with a right."

"It sounds thin, but I suppose we have no better option." Shane crossed his arms and knitted his brows together. "Should I drive the getaway vehicle?"

"I don't think so," said Bivens. "Your father is perfectly capable of driving. It would only slow things down to have someone in the driver's seat. That means more people will be trying to get in the remaining doors. Plus, we risk you getting caught if the plan doesn't work out."

Dan added, "Butterbean knows he'll be persona non grata after this, right? I mean, this ain't the kinda thing Hammer will let go."

"Assuming Hammer doesn't figure out my hand in the getaway, I'll try to help Butterbean escape. However, he knows that his role in this will cost him." Bivens nodded. "We'll all be fugitives when the smoke clears. At least until we get a new sheriff and a new mayor to exonerate us.

"I'm hoping we can get enough people to take a stand and guard the polls until we can have the elections. Once we have a new government, we can take down Hayes and all his cronies."

"Any idea how we'll get the word out about the elections without Hammer and Hayes shutting it down?" asked Dan.

"Folks around here know who they can trust. They know who's dirty and who's not. I'll put the word out to the other honest deputies once we have a date and a location." Bivens had a look of determination.

Shane agreed, "People aren't having this illegitimate tax. News of the elections will spread like wildfire, just like it did before. The residents of Jackson County are ready to fight. They just need a leader to rally behind.

"What about Fulton? What are we going to do with him?"

"I can tell Butterbean to leave his cuffs locked," answered Bivens. "I don't think we should leave him behind. Hayes and Hammer will exploit everything he knows about the group to look for a weakness to use in their counterattack."

Dan looked to Shane. "He's right."

"I have no illusions about that." Shane knew a war was coming. "I'm expecting his retribution to be swift and brutal."

"Fulton heard me say I was bringing the girls to the Tilley Creek area." Dan turned one of the shabby chairs around backward and took a seat at the table. "We won't be able to stay here long after the jailbreak. Shane found the cabin. Hammer will too. We probably shouldn't have even stayed here this long."

Bivens leaned back in his chair. "He's not expending the resources right now. But you're correct. After the escape, he'll have every man he can muster out here until he locates this place."

"I'm worried about dragging Fulton out to the distillery." Shane continued to pace the floor. "If he gets loose, he'll run straight to Hammer."

"We'll just have to make sure that doesn't happen," said Dan.

Eric Bivens stood up from the table. "I've got a few more preparations to make before tomorrow."

"Do you need us to do anything?" Shane asked.

"If you know where any guns are, get them. We're gonna need them. Otherwise, just sit tight and be ready to move when everyone gets here tomorrow." Bivens let himself out the door.

Dan stood up to latch the door behind Bivens. "Any idea where we can get guns? I'm pretty sure Hammer cleaned out all the firearms left at your compound."

"Maybe," said Shane. "Did you take your rifles when you left?"

"I did, but I left everything with Kari and the girls except for my rifle and pistol. They need to be able to defend themselves. Besides, what I took out to Pawpaw's wouldn't amount to a hill of beans up against Hammer and his men."

"Can I borrow your truck?"

"You're taking a big risk, driving around with the whole county looking for you." Dan reluctantly took out his keys. "You know Hammer has deputies posted all around your place."

"I know. But I'm going to come in over the hill, from Shiloh Creek Vistas."

"That's a gated community."

Shane lifted his shoulders. "I'll park at the bottom of the mountain and walk up."

"You be careful. It'll be dark soon."

"Then I best get a move on. Do you have a pack I can use to haul some ammo?"

Dan dug through his closet. "This one is old, but it's sturdy."

"Thanks." Shane opened the door. "Do you have a shovel lying around here?"

Dan pointed to the old shed out past the goat shelter. "Might find one in there. But watch your step. Ain't no tellin' what else you might find out there."

Shane grimaced hoping he wouldn't come across a snake who'd made his abode in the dilapidated old shack. Once there, he carefully peered inside and located a rusty shovel with a moldy wooden handle. "I guess this will have to do." He tossed it in the bed of Dan's truck and drove toward home.

***

The sun was setting by the time Shane excavated the rifles and pistols he'd buried with his father on the day prior. Shane took them all except one pistol. If they didn't live through the next week, the weapons would mean nothing to them anyway. He also took the gold coins he'd purchased at the beginning of the crisis. "It might be a while before we can come home. These could come in handy."

Shane picked his way through the briars getting back up the hill. He turned for one last look at his father's abandoned homestead. Suddenly, the kitchen light came on. Shane froze in his tracks. "Who could that be?" He waited for several minutes, trying to get a glimpse of the intruder. Finally, a shadowy figure passed rapidly by the window. Shane's mouth set in a hard line. "I can't see them from here." He waited for another chance to see the invader. Shane wrestled against his curiosity for a few minutes but eventually gave in to reason. "I should get going before I'm caught in the pitch-black forest."

***

The next morning, Shane and Dan bided their time impatiently in anticipation of any news concerning the first phase of the rescue mission. Shane paced by the window, peeking past the time-worn burlap curtains at regular intervals. He gripped the handle of his AR-15 so tightly his knuckles grew white. "Something's not right. They should have been here by now."

Dan sat anxiously on the edge of the old chair at the table, as if ready to spring like a cheetah at any moment. He glanced at his watch, then moved his rifle from his left side to his right. "The trial was set for 10:00. It's only 9:45. If Hammer and the mayor are expecting you to pull a rescue attempt, they'd probably want the window of opportunity as short as possible. They might not move the prisoners until 9:50. The courthouse isn't even five minutes from the jail. Give it until a quarter after before you have a conniption fit."

Shane said nothing, but rather pulled back the raggedy drapes with the flash suppressor of his rifle. He proceeded to pace and stare out the window toward the gravel driveway for the next thirty minutes. "It's 10:15. Is it time to worry now?"

Dan stood up and nervously pushed the chair under the table. "If it ain't, it's closer than it was a half hour ago." Dan's face was awash in concern. He joined Shane in staring out the window.

"What if this is a setup?" Shane turned to his companion. "What if Bivens sold us out?"

"I don't think he'd do that."

"What if he was caught? Do you think Hammer is above coerced interrogation?"

Dan scoffed, "Not at all."

"Then maybe it would be better if we weren't holed up inside the cabin like fish in a barrel if he comes here."

"Alright." Dan looked at Shane. "What do you have in mind?"

"Let's get our gear and wait out by the old goat

shelter. We can spot my dad and the others if they show up."

Dan nodded in agreement. "And if the sheriff comes, we can skedaddle up into the hills right quick."

Shane wasted no time. He loaded what he needed into his pack. "Do you have a good place to stash these extra guns?"

"I've got a loose floorboard in the closet. He'd find it if he took the time to look, but I'm betting he'll be more concerned with skinning your hide."

Shane followed Dan to the small bedroom with the extra weapons and ammunition. Once the guns were stowed, the two of them made haste in exiting the building.

The next hour was spent fretfully awaiting the arrival of either the escaped prisoners or Sheriff Hammer and his goons.

Shortly thereafter, a high-pitched buzz could be heard in the distance, almost like the sound of a hummingbird. The buzz quickly grew louder, until it more closely resembled a swarm of bees. Soon, Shane recognized the sound as the engine of a dirt bike. "It's a motorcycle. Get down!"

Dan lay prone in the tall spring grass. "Sounds like they're coming this way."

Shane watched. Finally, a robust male figure appeared atop a small motorbike, riding through the grass to avoid the gravel on his laborious trek to the old cabin.

"That's Butterbean!" exclaimed Dan. "If this was any other day, I'd be rolling on the floor laughing at the sight of him on the little bitty ol' dirt bike."

"He's alone," said Shane. "Let's go see what happened."

"Slow your roll, cowboy." Dan put his hand on Shane's arm. "Let's make sure he ain't got a posse on his tail."

Shane went back down on his stomach and watched as the hefty fellow gingerly got off the bike and marched up to the door of the cabin. "I don't see anyone else. I'll go see what happened. You stay here. Cover us if the sheriff's men show up and we have to make a run for it."

"I'll cover you. Ain't no point in trying to wait for Butterbean. He won't be outrunning nobody except a three-legged hound dog in these hills."

Shane slowly got up and approached the house. "Deputy Ritter," he called softly.

Butterbean spun around. With his high-pitched voice, he said, "Shane!"

"What happened?"

"Oh, it was awful. They got all the prisoners before they could get away. The sheriff blocked off the parking lot where the escape vehicle was parked. The sheriff got Eric, too."

"How did you get away?"

"I stuck the transport van in the ditch, got out, and ran into the neighborhood. My grandmama lived on Hemlock. I ran to her house and hid till they was all gone. My dirt bike was still in the garage and I had some old clothes in the closet."

Dan emerged from cover. "Hammer didn't know to look for you at your grandma's?"

"She died five years back. My daddy pays the taxes and cuts the yard once in a while. He keeps sayin' he's gonna sell it, but he just ain't got the heart to put it on the market."

Shane didn't want to offend the deputy, but he wasn't sure about the story. He turned to Dan. "Are you buying this?"

Dan looked Ritter over. "Butterbean couldn't tell a lie to save his life. As improbable as it sounds, I suppose it's remotely possible that he outran them."

"So now what?" Shane looked at Deputy Ritter.

"I guess Judge Lidke will still have the trial, even if they have to postpone it."

Dan added, "And Hammer will scour the countryside looking for us. We need to relocate."

"We need to put Plan B into action," said Shane.

"What's Plan B?" asked Butterbean.

With a grim face, Shane quickly explained the nuclear option, his only chance at rescuing his father and the others.

"That poor little girl!" said Butterbean.

"I know how bad it sounds." Shane felt horrible about what he had to do. "But the alternative is letting Pastor Joel, my father, Bobby, and Greg die. I'm sure Hayes can find enough rope to fit around Eric Bivens' neck for his role in all this, also."

Butterbean looked at the weathered porch of the old cabin. "You forgot about Mr. Farris."

"Fulton is the mole who let the mayor and Officer Hicks go free. I'm sure he'll be spared," Shane said harshly.

"Are you talking about Greg Harper, your sister's husband?" asked Butterbean.

"Yes, why?"

"He wasn't in the van. I don't think he's being

held at the jail at all."

"Oh?" Shane was confused. "Why not? Is he being kept somewhere else?"

"I don't believe he was on the docket. Is there any reason you can think of that he wouldn't be charged?"

"Only one." Shane's brow sunk low. "But we don't have time to sit around and speculate. We need to move. Butterbean, can we count on you to help us with our mission?"

"I'm awful sorry about your pa, but I can't do nothing to hurt that little girl."

"You won't have to. In fact, if you come along, it helps us make sure everything goes as planned, which will be much safer for Evelyn and her mother."

Butterbean looked at Dan apprehensively. "I guess."

Dan patted the heavy lawman on the back. "We ain't gonna hurt the girls, but Hayes will probably have some of his enforcers from Jackson Construction providing security for his lodge. I doubt them boys are going to let us do anything without a fight. You might have to shoot somebody."

"I'm a sworn officer of the law. I ain't got no problem with killin' the ones who need killin'."

"That's all I needed to know." Dan went inside the cabin. "Let me grab you some guns. I'll be right back."

CHAPTER 9

The bravest are surely those who have the clearest vision of what is before them, glory and danger alike, and yet notwithstanding, go out to meet it.

Thucydides

Shane sat up front with Dan in his two-door pickup truck. Due to spatial limitations in the cab, Butterbean rode in the bed of the truck.

Dan said, "We'll park on Paris Branch Road, then follow Henry Creek down a ways. From there, we can slip over the mountain and come right up on the back door."

"You think Hayes won't have men on the back side of the house?" asked Shane.

"He will, but not as many as he'll have on the front. If we can take them out and get inside the house, we can worry about the men in the front later."

"They'll be on us like flies on watermelon." Shane knew their chances were slim.

"Then we need to find the wife and daughter fast. Once we have them, the guards will stand down."

"Any idea what they'll use for a safe room once the shooting starts?"

"Upstairs master bedroom, I suspect. It's our best shot."

The more Shane thought about the half-baked plan, the less he liked it.

The team soon arrived at their destination. Dan pulled the truck off the road and into a natural blind. Once he'd exited the cab, Shane helped Butterbean out of the truck bed. "It's a long hike. Can you handle it?"

Butterbean already seemed winded from unloading himself. "I can do it. A few of us from work plays football on Sundays from time to time."

"I suppose that's something." Shane didn't feel convinced.

"Let's get a move on!" Dan led the team up the steep grade through the woods.

Shane kept pace with Dan. He considered what it was going to feel like when he became the vicious monster terrorizing the fragile little girl. He tried to get himself ready to look into her horrified eyes, knowing he was the source of yet more pain for the girl who'd already had such a hard life. A knot formed in his throat. Guilt and shame seeped into his mind, threatening his resolve.

"Y'all wait up!" Butterbean struggled to speak. "I need to sit down for a minute."

Dan paused to let the overweight deputy catch up. He looked at Shane's remorse-filled eyes. "You gonna be alright?"

Shane turned away from his friend. "I'm good."

"I don't know about that. You need to be fully convinced that you're doing the right thing when you go into something like this. Anything less will get you killed. It will get us all killed."

Shane bravely glanced up to his companion's eyes. "I'm trying. But I have to admit, I wish there were another way. I'm not looking forward to this."

"Me neither, but I think you need to change the channel," said Dan.

"What do you mean?" asked Shane.

"I'm talking about that scene you're playing in your head. You need to put on a different movie. Try rolling the one where your daddy's head is getting slipped into a noose come tomorrow morning."

Shane set his teeth together with a renewed sense of determination. "That helps. Thanks."

"You ready, bigun?" Dan asked Butterbean.

Butterbean huffed for air. With his face flushed white with red blotches, he nodded adamantly and continued his ascent.

The team had to break three more times before reaching the summit but eventually arrived. Shane lay still with his rifle cradled in his arms. He looked on at the wall of windows facing out over the mountains. "I bet they've got one heck of a view."

"That's good. Maybe they won't see us little vermin down here in the brush, crawling around on our bellies." Dan took out his small pair of field binoculars to inspect the house.

"What do you see?" Shane looked through the scope of his rifle.

Dan scanned the area. "I count two guards downstairs, hanging out on the patio furniture like they was on vacation. I see two more, upstairs on the other side of those big glass windows. Looks like they're watching a movie. This might be easier than we thought."

"Let's not start counting unhatched chickens," warned Shane. "Butterbean, do you think you can hit one of the men on the couch inside the window?"

"If he was a deer I could hit him." The heavy deputy spied his target through the scope of his AR-15.

"Why if he were a deer?" Dan asked. "Because you could eat him?"

The deputy frowned at the brash humor.

"I'm just foolin' with you," laughed Dan. "Pretend he's a big 'ol juicy bacon cheeseburger from Kostas."

"I'll hit him," Butterbean scowled.

"Can you hit the one downstairs on the left?" Dan put down his binoculars and looked at Shane.

"I think so." Shane nodded.

"This is for all the marbles. You need to take him out." Dan raised his rifle.

"Okay. I'll hit my mark." Shane steadied the gun.

"That last one is going to be running around like

a chicken with his head cut off after we kill all his buddies. We'll team up on him once the others are down." Dan took aim.

"Hold up! There's the girl!" Shane quickly placed his hand on Dan's shoulder. He watched as a young girl navigated through the living area where the guards were watching television. She utilized forearm crutches and continued on to the kitchen where she retrieved a drink from the refrigerator.

Shane's stomach sank. The feeling of guilt returned like a haunting specter. Dan seemed to notice. "Remember why you're doing this, buddy. If we had any other options, we wouldn't be here."

"Yeah." Shane watched with an empathetic gaze. "Still, we have to wait until she's out of the room."

"No problem." Dan continued looking through his scope while the girl returned the way she'd came. "Alright, get ready. On three. One, two, three!"

All three rifles popped simultaneously, each taking down their intended targets. Shane took aim at the fourth guard who'd instinctively dropped to the floor and was quickly crawling away from the window. He took a shot but was sure he'd missed.

"He's gone now, boys. We'll have to rush 'em." Dan sprung up from his concealed position. "Butterbean, I need you to run like you've never run before."

Shane charged across the lawn with Dan. Butterbean made a concerted effort to keep up. Shane smashed out the glass of the downstairs door with the stock of his rifle. Dan reached in and unlocked it. "We need to get to that room where the girl went."

Shane followed him inside and up the stairs. "She went to the left. That limits our search."

Gunfire rang out when they topped the stairs. Shane drooped to the floor. "Where is he?"

Dan pointed to the other side of the wall of the stairwell. "In the kitchen, I think."

Shane nodded. "Rush him?"

"Yep." Dan got ready to move.

Butterbean finally arrived, gasping for breath. He looked at Shane and Dan. "Are we taking a break?"

"Not yet." Shane led the charge around the corner. He and Dan both unleashed a volley of rifle fire on the remaining guard.

Shane changed his magazine. "The guards from out front of the house will be headed this way. We need to find the girl."

"Come on, Butterbean!" Dan yelled and followed Shane down the hall.

The three of them checked each room.

"She's gone!" decried Butterbean.

"She probably went upstairs with her mother when the shooting started." Shane led the way to the top floor. He heard the sound of men coming in the front door.

"Roland is down!" yelled one.

"Secure the master bedroom," called another.

"That's it at the end of the hall." Dan pointed straight ahead.

The three men charged toward the door.

"I'll bust it open!" volunteered Butterbean.

Dan and Shane stood to the side as the hefty fellow slammed his body weight against the door which readily gave way. Shane rushed in and scanned the area for hostiles. He saw an older woman pointing a pistol at him. "Don't do it. There's no need for you or your daughter to die. If you pull that trigger, you'll make her an orphan."

Dan trained his scope on the woman's head. Butterbean slammed the door and held it shut behind them. The woman gripped the pistol tightly, aiming for Shane's face. "I'll take at least one of you with me when I go."

"And you'll leave Evelyn all alone in a hostile world," Shane replied.

"She'll still have her father."

"Oh no, his fate is sealed," Shane countered. "But you, you have a choice."

A guard from outside yelled through the door, "Mrs. Hayes? Are you alright in there?"

Shane stepped closer to the woman, knowing that he had to get that pistol away from her or they were all dead. He called to the guard. "We have Mrs. Hayes and Evelyn. Put down your guns, or they'll die and so will you." Shane gently took the pistol from the woman's hand. He nodded to let her know that she was doing the best thing for her daughter. "Work with me here. I promise you and Evelyn will be fine if you do."

"Put 'em down, Gabe," Mrs. Hayes said to the guard outside.

"I don't think that's what the mayor would want," said the guard.

"Do it, Gabe. Or you'll get us all killed," she yelled.

Shane addressed the guard, "Gabe, I need you to

pull the laces out of the other guards' boots. Then I need you to tie them up tight. I'm holding you responsible if any of the knots aren't good enough. It will cost the lives of you and the man you improperly secured if any of them look like they could wiggle free."

No one called back.

"I think they left," said Butterbean.

"That's what I would've done," Dan added. "It was worth a try." He patted Shane on the shoulder. "We'll get Mrs. Hayes ready for transport if you want to find the girl."

Shane split off toward the bathroom where he heard sobbing. He knocked gently. "Evelyn, unlock the door so we don't have to shoot the doorknob off and risk injuring you."

He waited for a second but heard no compliance, only more sobbing. He rattled the knob. "Last chance. We're coming in, one way or the other." After some cumbersome clanking, he heard the lock release. Shane opened the door calmly. The girl sat on the edge of the giant whirlpool tub, still crying, with her crutches in her hand.

"Evelyn, I need you to get some things together. You're going to be staying with us for a while."

"Why? You're going to kill us anyway."

Shane felt sick at his stomach over what he was doing. He took a seat next to the frail girl. He whispered near her ear. "I'll tell you a secret. I'm not going to hurt you."

"What about my mom?"

He shook his head and forced a smile. "I'm not going to hurt her either."

"And my dad?" She struggled against the palsy to turn her head and look Shane in the eyes.

Shane didn't want to add lying to his list of sins for the day. But neither did he want to further upset the girl. He lost his ability to fake a smile. "That's up to your father. He's going to kill my dad and a lot of my friends tomorrow morning unless you can help me convince him not to."

Her reply sounded bitter. "I guess I don't have a choice." She let her muscles relax and her head bobbed away.

Shane swallowed the knot forming in his throat. "Come on. Let's get your things." Shane helped her to stand but let her walk on her own.

Evelyn bravely worked her crutches through the door and into the bedroom.

"It's going to be okay, sweetie," her mother assured.

Evelyn fought to fix her gaze on Mrs. Hayes. Her mouth contorted but her speech was crystal clear. "I hope so, mama."

"Butterbean and I will sweep the house. You get the girls packed." Dan finished off a knot around Mrs. Hayes' wrists. "Hopefully we'll find a vehicle in the garage. Then we won't have to expose ourselves to snipers by going outside without some form of cover."

Shane nodded and went into the closet to get a bag. He put her cell phone and a change of clothes in a shoulder bag. "What does Evelyn need?"

The young girl answered for herself. Even though she had little control of her expressions, her snark came shining through. "Evelyn needs her bear and the book she's reading. They're both on my bed."

"She also needs her medication and some clean clothes," her mother added.

Shane escorted the two of them down the stairs, collected Evelyn's things in the shoulder bag and continued down to the garage.

Dan pointed to the collection of long-term storage foods in large white plastic buckets. "Any of this stuff look familiar?"

"This is all from my dad's cabin." He pointed to the big black SUV. "Fit as much of it as we can in the back of the Yukon."

"Do y'all have enough guns where we're going?" Butterbean asked.

"Not really," Shane answered.

"Maybe we should get the guns from the guards we shot," Butterbean said.

"Make it snappy," Shane replied. "Gabe and the other guards are most likely lying in wait for us outside and they've probably called for backup by now."

Five minutes later, the vehicle was loaded up. Dan drove, Butterbean rode shotgun, with Shane guarding Evelyn and Gina Hayes. Dan revved the engine before pushing the button to open the garage. The large metal door opened at a glacial speed. "Come on!" Dan urged the mechanical door to hurry.

Once it opened, Dan punched the gas and the tires spun. The Yukon jetted out of the garage. Immediately, gunfire erupted.

"Are they crazy?" Shane asked as he rolled down

his window to return fire. "They could hit the hostages!" He let out a barrage of rifle fire, then turned back to Gina and Evelyn. "Get down! Get as close to the floorboard as possible!"

Gina shielded her daughter by lying over top of her.

Shane and Butterbean exchanged shots with the guards while Dan sped out of the long driveway to the road. Soon, all the weapons fell silent. Shane inspected Gina and Evelyn to see if they'd been hit. Next, he gave himself a once-over.

Dan raced the vehicle down the mountain. "Butterbean, I'm going to need you to do a Chinese fire drill with me."

"You want me to drive?" asked the large man.

"Yep. I caught one in the leg."

"You're shot?" asked Shane.

"Afraid so," he answered. "This has to be fast, Butterbean. I'll throw her in park and we'll both bail out. You gotta move. They could be coming after us."

"Okay!" Butterbean nodded.

Dan stopped at the bottom of the hill and put the SUV in park. He stepped out of the vehicle and collapsed to the ground. Shane pointed at Gina Hayes. "Don't move!"

"Seriously?" She shrugged her arms which were tied behind her back.

Shane quickly got out to assist Dan to the passenger's seat. Blood was coming out of his thigh. Once Dan was in the seat, Shane pulled his belt off and wrapped it under Dan's leg. He tightened it and handed the end for Dan to hold.

"Keep tension on this."

Dan winced in pain. "Yep."

Shane slammed his door and slapped the back of Butterbean's seat. "Go, go, go!"

The deputy hit the gas pedal. "Where? Where?"

"Dan, where are we going, pal?" asked Shane.

"74 all the way to Marble. Then 141 to Vengeance Creek. There's an old forest service road near the end. It's unmarked, so you'll really have to look for it."

"You better check this thing for a GPS locator," Dan added.

"I have no idea how to do that," Shane replied.

"It's probably up under the dash or center console. Once we're about 10 miles out, pull off to the side. I'll walk you through it."

Shane worried that Dan would go unconscious and neither he nor Butterbean would know what to look for. "Let's make it three miles."

Butterbean pointed to an antique shop coming up on the side of the road. "What about right here?"

"That will work," said Shane. "Pull in behind the building."

Butterbean complied with Shane's directions. "Okay, now what?"

Dan replied, "Look up under the center console. At the very bottom should be a shiny metal box. That's the OnStar unit."

Butterbean breathed heavily as he got out and tried to maneuver himself to see under the dash. "I see it. There's all kinds of wires going every which way."

"You've probably got two different cable

harnesses going in plus a single wire by itself."

"I see it."

"Pull out the single wire. That's the antenna. They can't track us without that being plugged in."

"What if I pull out the wrong wire?"

"Just don't," said Dan.

"Okay, it's out." Butterbean sounded unsure of his actions.

"Turn the key. If it still starts, you did it right."

Butterbean turned the ignition switch and the engine started. "It works!"

"Good job, let's get out of here!" Shane pointed forward.

Dan took a deep breath as if in great pain. "If I don't make it, tell Kari and Scott that I love 'em."

CHAPTER 10

The supreme art of war is to subdue the enemy without fighting.

Sun Tzu

Shane and the others arrived at the safe house near Murphy roughly an hour later. Butterbean carried Dan to the small porch of a dilapidated old shotgun house. The antique dwelling was long and narrow. Rust coated the metal roof. Paint which had once been white peeled and flaked off of warped wooden boards.

Shane assisted Gina and Evelyn in exiting the vehicle. Julianna and Shane's sister, Angela, were the first to emerge from the weathered old structure. They each held AR-15s. Kari Ensley was next to run out of the house. She embraced her husband. "Dan! You're shot."

"Don't make a fuss over it. I don't want to upset Scott." He cringed in pain.

Soon, all the residents of Pawpaw's distillery came outside to see what was going on. Tonya, Maggie Farris, and Mrs. Perkins assisted Kari and Butterbean with getting Dan into the house where they could care for his wound.

Pastor Joel's wife, Elizabeth stared with wide eyes at her niece and sister-in-law who were in Shane's custody. "What are you doing, Shane?"

"Ma'am. We don't have any other choice. The mayor is going to hang Pastor Joel along with the others tomorrow morning if we can't get him to reconsider."

"Hang them?" She seemed more distressed by this revelation than the sight of her niece as a hostage. "But even so, this isn't right!"

"I appreciate your concern, but it's not your decision." He turned to his sister. "Angela, can you escort the pastor's wife into the house? This is our only hope of getting Dad back."

"Elizabeth, come on. Let's get something to drink." Angela attempted to put her arm on Elizabeth's.

The pastor's wife jerked her arm away from Angela. "I'm not one of your prisoners. You can't just tell me to go away!"

Shane deeply regretted everything about this day. He did not want to pile on more transgressions by yelling at Elizabeth, but he could not let her jeopardize his mission. He raised his voice. "You're not my prisoner right now, but if you get in my way, I'll do whatever I have to. You may be more concerned with treating everyone nice than you are about your husband's imminent demise, but I've already crossed the Rubicon. I have no limit to how far I'm willing to go to bring my father home! I suggest you allow Angela to get you out of my path!"

He had no intentions of hurting Elizabeth, nor her niece, nor her sister-in-law. But the theatrics were necessary to ensure it never came to that. She heeded the warning and went away with Angela.

"For what it's worth, I understand why you're handling things the way you are. I don't blame you for your tactics." Only Julianna remained at Shane's side. "What are you going to do with these two?"

"I don't know. Is there a good outbuilding that could serve as a holding cell?"

Julianna nodded toward the shotgun house. "An old still is back through those woods. It's set up inside a huge barn. Behind it is a wooden grain silo. I guess that's where they kept the corn for production. It doesn't have a lock to speak of, but I suppose we could rig something up."

"Let's check it out." Shane waved to Gina and Evelyn. "Come on, ladies."

The short path through the woods soon opened up to a tremendous red wooden barn with multiple stove pipes coming out of the old tin roof. "Wow! What's all of that?"

"Ventilation for the stills."

"Stills? As in more than one?"

"Six," Julianna replied.

"Dan led me to believe this was a small operation, only used for cough syrup and rubbing alcohol."

"Then they had a funny way of branding it. The barn has cases of empty bottles with labels on them. They say, *Pawpaw's Finest Sour Mash, Secret Family Recipe*. And if it was for cough syrup, they were putting out enough for the whole country to have bronchitis at the same time."

Shane examined the old silo. He looked to his hostages. "Ladies, go ahead and make yourselves comfortable. We'll get this place cleaned up for you and see what we can do about getting you a mattress." He felt terrible about confining Evelyn in such horrific quarters.

"She can't sleep in here," protested her mother.

Shane seized upon the opportunity, in hopes of both getting the young girl out of the situation and ensuring cooperation by the mother. "Okay, if I let her stay with her aunt, can I count on you to not give us any problems?"

"I'm locked up in a grain silo. What harm can I cause?"

"You could be difficult," he said. "Then I promise, that will result in me being less accommodative. For your daughter's sake, I hope you won't test my resolve on this."

"I'll play along. But I want to see her every day," said the mother.

Shane nodded. "Hopefully we'll have this all sorted out by tomorrow. But if not, I'll make sure you have daily visitations, as long as you're on your best behavior."

"Mom?" Even through her distorted facial expressions, Evelyn's concern showed over being separated from her mother.

"It's okay, honey. You go with Aunt Elizabeth. I'll be fine here. And I'll see you later. I love you."

"I love you, too." Evelyn's head went left, then down. She maneuvered her forearm crutches and turned back toward the trail through the woods.

"Can you watch the door until I find a way to lock it?" Shane asked.

Julianna looked him over. "Sure."

"Come on, Evelyn," he said, but the girl was already on her way.

Shane caught up to her. "I need some assurances from you also. You're not going to run off, are you?"

She paused to look at him, her chin angled up and slightly to the side. "You never know. After all, I am a lightning-fast sprinter."

Shane smiled nervously.

"But I'm also a professional MMA fighter. The only reason any of you are still breathing is because I'm choosing to let you live." Evelyn turned back to the trail. "At least for now."

He'd forgotten about her flamboyant snark. "I'll sleep with one eye open."

Once back to the narrow shotgun house, Shane found the pastor's wife and explained the arrangement. She agreed to look after her niece and to follow Shane's lead. Next, Shane looked in on Dan who was being cared for in the small kitchen. Bloody rags lay in the sink. Maggie Farris used an old worn-out mop to clean the floor under the work area. Dan sat atop the simple wooden table. He still seemed to be in pain but was conscious and alert.

Angela walked out of the kitchen into the living room. "I think he's going to be okay. Did you get everything worked out with your . . . guests?"

Shane decided not to mention the speculation about her husband being the mole. Even if it turned out to be true, it could have a detrimental effect on their relationship at a time when he needed all the support he could get. "Yeah, I think I've got it all sorted out. I need a lock for the silo. I'm using that to keep the mayor's wife locked up."

"I saw some tools in the old woodshed behind the house."

"Lead the way." He motioned for his sister to go out first.

"We'll go out the front door. To get out the back, you have to go through the kitchen and both bedrooms. I can see why shotgun houses aren't in style anymore."

"How are all of you fitting in this small house?" he asked.

"We aren't. Elizabeth Hayes and Mom were sharing the back bedroom. Maggie and Mrs. Perkins are sharing the middle. The rest of us are sleeping in the barn. I guess the young girl will sleep with her aunt and Mom will take the couch. I hope we can go home soon. It's hard to use an outhouse in the middle of the night without wondering if there is a snake or something down there."

"Where's Cole?"

"When we heard the vehicle coming up the dirt road, we thought it could be trouble. Julianna sent him and Scott to a place in the barn where they hide." Angela opened the door to the tattered shed. "Kari is out there with them now. She thought it would be best for Scott not to see Dan's leg looking so bad."

"Yeah, Cole doesn't need to see it either. The kitchen looks like a slaughterhouse right now." Shane found a stick to clear out the cobwebs before entering. Using the same stick, he poked around looking for something to use for a lock. Dated pieces of farm machinery, odds-and-ends, and tools from a bygone era were stuffed in every dusty nook and moldy cranny of the crumbling outbuilding. A rusted coffee can held various nuts and bolts piled to the top. Shane tipped it over with his foot and sorted through its contents with the stick. "Here's an old screw-on shed door latch. It's got a place for a lock, but I don't see anything to secure it with."

Angela peered inside. She picked up a wooden-handled screwdriver. "Could you stick this in the place for the lock? She's not going to be able to open it."

Shane's brows dipped low. "She's not, but I'm worried about Elizabeth or Evelyn sneaking out there and setting her free. I suppose it will do for now. I'll keep looking. There's bound to be a lock and key around here somewhere."

Once the latch was installed as a temporary means of keeping the mayor's wife secure, the moment of truth came. It was time for Shane to contact the mayor. He took Gina's phone, which he'd removed from the shoulder bag, opened the silo door, and snapped a picture of her sitting in the dingy grain storage area. He closed the door, attached the picture to a text and sent it to the mayor. The text said, *This is the last picture of your wife alive you'll see if the prisoners aren't released in one hour.*

Shane stared at the phone, but no reply came. He paced around the silo, hoping the plan would succeed. If it didn't, his father and friends would die.

CHAPTER 11

Then the Lord said unto Moses, Go in unto Pharaoh, and tell him, Thus saith the Lord God of the Hebrews, Let my people go, that they may serve me.

Exodus 9:1

Shane returned to the house where he found Julianna still on guard duty. She sat on a fallen pine log with her rifle in hand, watching the road. "Mind if I have a seat?" he asked.

She looked him over, then turned her attention back to the road. "It's a free country. Or at least it used to be."

"We brought some supplies which the mayor had stolen from my dad's cabin." He sat on the other end of the log.

"Yeah, Butterbean told us. Your mom and Mrs. Perkins are cooking up some dinner for everyone. We didn't bring much out here. Kari and I have killed a few squirrels. We've been looking for deer but haven't seen any. I was getting worried; not for me, but for Cole." She glanced at him with the first look of tenderness he'd seen from her since he came back. "Thanks, for bringing the food."

"Oh, sure. I'm sorry things got so messed up and you had to come out here with Cole." He turned in such a way that inched him closer to her position on the log.

She eyed his knee which was only a foot away from her leg as if it were invading her private space. Julianna stood up but said nothing. She focused on the empty road and ignored him.

Shane wished he'd not been so hasty, wanted the awkwardness to vanish. The uncomfortable moment met its demise when Gina's phone vibrated in his pocket. It was a text from the mayor and the reply had come almost exactly one hour since he'd initiated contact. Shane read the text aloud. "You're bluffing. Paul and the others will hang tomorrow at 10:00 AM. Come on down. I've still got rope for one more."

Julianna's expression turned to compassion. "What are you going to do?"

"I don't know." Shane felt horrible. He had few options, and none of them were good. "I'll see you later."

Shane walked back toward the dilapidated house. He looked to Heaven. "God, I'm in a jam. I could really use some help. I'm already so ashamed of what I've had to do today. Now—it looks like I'm going to have to do something even worse. Please help me."

Shane allowed his gaze to fall to the leaf-covered path below his feet. He trudged up the narrow stairs like a man condemned to die. Only it was not his own death he was so concerned with.

In the living room, Dan lay on the couch, resting soundly. His wife and son sat nearby keeping vigil.

"How is he?" Shane whispered.

"I think he's going to be okay." Kari smiled.

Shane tiptoed past to the kitchen. Tonya and Maggie Farris were working quietly to put away the supplies brought from the mayor's house. Mrs. Perkins stirred a pot simmering over a wood burning stove.

"I wouldn't spend too much time worrying about putting all that stuff in the cupboards, Mom," said Shane. "I'm not planning to be here long."

Tonya replied, "We're tripping over each other in this tiny house. It has to go someplace, even if we leave tonight." She handed him a large can. "This is your father's stash alright. Who else would buy powdered tomato sauce?"

Shane inspected the metal can filled with dehydrated tomato powder. Suddenly, a thought hit him, as if a voice inside were speaking, inaudibly, but altogether understandable. "Do we have a can opener?"

Tonya handed him the multitool in her pocket. "Another one of your father's purchases. This one has proved to be quite handy. Keep the tomato sauce but bring my multitool back."

"Thanks." Shane turned to leave.

"How's it going anyway?" His mother's voice sounded confident, as if her capable son had everything under control. "With bringing him home, I mean?"

He turned back hoping his eyes wouldn't betray the bumbling mess he'd made of the situation. "Good. I'll have it all worked out soon." His contrived smile faded instantly when he turned around to continue his mission.

Shane walked through the wooded path to the barn. Strolling through, he saw Butterbean. "Hey, what's going on?"

"Your mama gave me an old quilt. I was trying to set me up a little sleeping area. I figured someone would need to keep watch tonight. I'm plum tuckered right now. Thought if I caught a few winks, I could take first shift this evening."

"That's a good plan," Shane said. "Have you seen any locks laying around here?"

"There's all kinds of mismatch parts in a wood crate in that little storage room back there." Butterbean pointed to the rear of the giant barn.

"Thanks." Shane strode past giant copper pots, streaked green and black from decades of oxidation and dust. Inside the room, Shane found an antique brass padlock. A piece of baling twine held two keys attached to the historical artifact. He untied the knot in the twine and tried placing one of the keys into the lock. "A little WD-40 and we'd be in business." He looked but found no such substance. He did, however, find a dust-covered oil can. He picked it up and smiled at feeling that it still had something in it. A few drops of the oil, some jiggling, and the lock popped open. Shane placed the lock and keys in his pocket, picked up the can of tomato powder, and continued to the silo.

Shane removed the screwdriver holding the latch to the holding cell. He opened the door and walked in to see a dejected woman. Gina Hayes had been the pinnacle of small-town society. Yet here she sat on a dank and dingy grain bin floor. It was not entirely unlike Shane's own dissension from opulence and luxury. But that is where their commonality ended, he supposed; unless one considered that it was the actions of Wallace Hayes who'd caused their two paths to cross in the first place.

Shane sat the tomato sauce on the floor.

"What's this?"

"It's Evelyn's final chance at not being an orphan."

"Explain."

Shane drew his pistol and squatted near the captive. "The mayor thinks I'm bluffing. He thinks I won't kill either of you. So, he's going to hang my father and my friends tomorrow morning."

She shook her head. "That idiot!"

"He's partly right. Evelyn has never done anything to deserve this. I wouldn't kill her."

"And me? What crime have I committed?"

"You're an accessory to every one of your husband's wrongs."

"You can't tie me to any of his dealings. He doesn't ask my counsel or permission."

"Perhaps not, but you've stuck by him."

"What would you have me do? Rat him out to the FBI for corruption?"

"That's one option, sure. But to keep your daughter around a man everyone knows is a criminal; it's negligence, bordering on child abuse. Nefarious behavior, like that of your husband's, is always accompanied by violence. What do you think the job title is of those men guarding your house? What do you think the nature of their employment was prior to the collapse?"

She looked at the dirt as if not willing to incriminate herself with a statement.

"They were enforcers." Shane made a circular motion with the barrel of the gun indicating to Gina Hayes' present circumstances. "By staying at his side, you ensured that a day like this would eventually come. It was inevitable."

Her voice betrayed her deep regret. "Why are you lecturing me? What good can come of it? Do you simply enjoy hearing yourself dispense moral reprimands from a place of power? Don't think you are so different. I wonder what your adoring fans would think if they knew you were capable of terrorizing a poor little girl who has fought her entire life through speech and physical therapy just to walk across the room or ask for a drink of water."

The statement jabbed Shane in the heart. "That world is gone. In this world, I'm being as companionate as the new reality will allow."

"Tell yourself whatever you like. I'm in no position to argue." She crossed her arms and turned away from him.

"I'm willing to kill you if that's what it takes to bring my father home."

Her voice cracked. "Why are you tormenting me? If that's what you've come here to do, why not just get it over with? You're not a good person, Shane Black. You can lie to the people who watch Country Music Television, but you and me, we know who you really are."

"As easy as you're making it for me to pull this trigger, I still have one motivating factor encouraging me to find an alternate solution."

"I'm listening." She kept her back toward him. "I'm the dictionary definition of a captive audience."

"If I kill you, Evelyn will be an orphan. As I said before, the mayor has to die. If you both die, she'll be forced to live out her days with her aunt and uncle. They happen to be members of my compound. It will be a prison sentence for her to live here with me, her parents' killer."

Gina shook her head. Shane could tell she hated to think of such a future for Evelyn. "So, what's the alternative?"

Shane picked up the can of tomato powder with one hand and held his pistol with the other. "The alternative is that we fake your execution. It has to be messy and it has to look good. I'll snap a picture of your dead body lying in a pool of blood and hope the mayor buys it. You better pray he falls for it, too."

"Why is that?"

Shane tightened his jaw. "Because if he doesn't, I'm going to send him your head in a box. And I can't think of any way to mock that up."

Gina seemed to need no further convincing of Shane's willingness to do exactly what he'd threatened. "Okay. What do you want me to do?"

"First of all, I'm going to mix up some tomato sauce. We'll tie your hands up with baling twine and rub dirt all over your face and arms. When the mayor looks at this picture, he needs to think your last minutes on earth were not pleasant ones. Hopefully, he'll want to spare Evelyn of the same fate and let my father go."

"I'll cooperate. Just tell me how to proceed."

CHAPTER 12

And Pharaoh rose up in the night, he, and all his servants, and all the Egyptians; and there was a great cry in Egypt; for there was not a house where there was not one dead. And he called for Moses and Aaron by night, and said, Rise up, and get you forth from among my people, both ye and the children of Israel; and go, serve the Lord, as ye have said.

Exodus 12:30-31

Thursday evening, Shane examined the gruesome picture he'd just attached to the text message. Julianna crinkled her nose as she looked on. The image depicted Gina Hayes lying lifeless on the floor of the grain bin. Her corpse appeared discarded in a puddle of blood which was soaking into the hard earth beneath her cold body. Her face was marred as if brutally beaten, her arms soiled and bound behind her back. Shane shivered at the grotesqueness of the scene. It had undoubtedly produced the desired effect in his own mind. He could only hope that it would do the same for Wallace Hayes.

Shane read the accompanying text aloud as an edit. "Your failure to comply with my demand has cost Gina her life. I'd like to tell you that it was quick and painless, that she died peacefully, but nothing could be farther from the truth. Her violent death and the agonizing last hours of her life are on your conscience. You'll have to live with the fact that you could have prevented it and chose not to.

"To say it will be worse for Evelyn is an understatement. Her final torment will be tenfold what Gina's was. She'll have to endure it while looking at her mother's stiff cadaver lying on the floor in front of her. It's not something I'm looking forward to, but if you again underestimate my determination to get my father back, the next picture I send will be your daughter's dead body stacked on top of her mother's." Shane looked up at Julianna, his eyes pleading for her to not think him a soulless villain.

"It's harsh, but anything less and you risk him not falling for it," she said. "Then you really will have to kill her."

Shane nodded, looked at the macabre visual once more, took a deep breath and clicked the send icon.

"I hope it works."

A reply came almost immediately. I'll let your group go. Tell me where to meet you for the exchange.

Shane quickly entered his response. It doesn't work like that. You let my group go, Deputy Bivens included. Once we're convinced that they haven't been followed, I'll tell you where to find Evelyn.

You expect me to trust you? Absolutely not! The mayor's answer came rapidly.

Then I'll send you video of Evelyn's execution. If I have to listen to her screaming, begging for mercy like her mother did, then so should you. Stand by. I'll have it to you in about ten minutes.

Julianna looked on. Her eyes flicked up at Shane as if to make sure he'd not turned from Dr. Jekyll to Mr. Hyde. Shane hated this debut into his acting career and hoped he'd never be asked to give an encore performance.

Seconds later, the mayor replied. You win. I'll have them in a transport van within the hour. Don't double-cross me on this. I'll skin you alive.

A sense of relief washed over Shane like a cold breeze in the middle of August. "That's it. He's going to let them go!"

"You better save the victory lap," Julianna warned. "This is a positive development, but it's far from over."

"I need to go back to Dan's hunting cabin to meet them. They'll never find this place without directions."

"By yourself?" Julianna asked.

Shane thought he detected a note of concern but

didn't dare mention it. "I'll take Butterbean."

"I could go," she said. "If you want."

As much as Shane relished the thought of being with her, he could not allow it. "No. You have to stay here, for Cole." He handed her Gina's phone. "Besides, you're the only one who can keep this bluff going if the mayor pulls a fast one and decides to go back on his agreement."

"I'm glad you're so confident in my ability to play the part of a ruthless witch."

He fought a smile. "You understand what needs to be done and you're not afraid to do it. It's a compliment."

"Oh—then, thanks . . ." Julianna seemed to be holding back a grin. "I guess."

***

Shane dropped off Butterbean at Dan's truck on the way back to the hunting cabin. "Stay close. I don't think he'll risk pulling anything when he's desperately trying to get his daughter back, but you never know.

"I'll be right behind you."

Shane waited for him to get in the vehicle then drove the Yukon toward Dan's old hunting cabin. He parked behind the house in the woods. If the mayor did decide to double-cross them, Butterbean would need a vehicle in order to escape. Shane had no intention of abandoning the deputy, so fleeing on foot was not an option.

"Are we going to wait for them in the house?" Butterbean exited the two-door pickup truck.

"No. We'll watch from the forest, near the Yukon."

Butterbean followed Shane to the selected observation point. Shane checked his watch. "It's been an hour. Something isn't right."

"What are you going to do if he doesn't let them go?" Butterbean asked.

Shane didn't want to answer that question. He could barely stand being in his own skin because of the atrocities he'd already committed. "Let's just pray that he does."

The minutes passed and Shane grew more anxious. Finally, he heard a vehicle approaching. A van drove up the dirt road. "Butterbean, get down!"

The two of them lay low in the brush watching to see what would happen. Shane saw the driver's side door open and his father step out. He grabbed Butterbean's arm and fought the urge to run out to greet him.

"Doesn't look like anyone is home." Pastor Joel exited the passenger's side.

Eric Bivens came out the sliding side door. "They wouldn't be sitting around the house playing cards anyway. They'd be hiding out, making sure this isn't an ambush."

Shane whispered to Butterbean. "Stay here. If we get hit, provide cover fire until we can get to the woods."

Butterbean readied his weapon. "Okay, I'll do it."

Shane slowly got up as he watched Bobby and the other members of his group emerge from the van. He carefully left the concealment of the tree line.

His father was the first to spot him. "Shane?"

"Hey, Dad." He approached Paul cautiously. "You guys alone?"

"As far as I can tell. We stopped and looked for GPS devices. We didn't find any, but Hayes could have something in one of the tires or anywhere. I'd feel better about it if I had found a device."

Shane looked over the vehicle. "We've got Dan's truck and an SUV which should be clean. We can ditch the van. We won't need it to get where we're going."

"The mayor seemed pretty unhappy about not getting to hang us. You must have some pretty serious leverage over him."

Shane was thrilled to have his dad back but couldn't get past the remorse of what he'd done to bring about his release. He hugged his father. "Yeah."

Paul patted him on the back. "I guess you'll tell me when you feel like it."

"It's a long story. We need to get going." Shane motioned toward the tree line. "Butterbean, you can come on out. Bring up the Yukon."

Shane eyed Fulton. "Do you still trust him? If he's the one who let the mayor go, we'll be jeopardizing Mom, Angela, and the others if we bring him to the hideout."

Pastor Joel stood nearby. "Fulton is not your rat."

"Then who is?" Shane looked at him untrustingly.

Pastor Joel nodded to Paul, as if it were not his

place to say.

Paul replied, "We think it was Greg."

Shane looked at the ground. "I was afraid of that."

"Did you say anything to Angela?" asked Paul.

"No, I didn't know for sure. I didn't want to upset her if it weren't true." Shane opened the door to the Yukon. "You and Pastor Joel ride with us." Shane pointed to Bobby. "Good to see you, big guy. Why don't you drive the transport van? We'll dump it on the side of the road somewhere. Then you can jump in the back of the pickup. Eric, you drive Dan's truck. Fulton will ride with you. Keys are in the ignition."

The group loaded up quickly and moved out.

On the way back, Shane let Butterbean drive so he could explain to his father and Pastor Joel the lengths he'd gone to in order to secure their release.

"You did what you had to. I, for one, appreciate it," said the pastor.

"I'm afraid your wife doesn't feel the same way," Shane replied.

"She's a woman, and naturally wired more as a nurturer than a warrior." Pastor Joel chuckled. "If she'd have been a big, burly, battle-axe-wielding broad, there's a good chance I'd never have married her. We balance each other out. Deep down, she appreciates what you did. At least I hope she does."

"If there were another way, I'm sure you would have found it." Paul reached over the back seat to give Shane's shoulder a squeeze. "The second we let them go, it's over. He'll hunt us down like dogs and we have no leverage."

"Then we should have the elections before we set them free," said the pastor.

"Eric Bivens thinks he can get the word out pretty quickly." Shane turned around to face the men in the back seat. "I know elections are usually held on a Tuesday, but I'm not sure we can stall that long. What do you think about Saturday?"

"Having elections on Saturday is a significant breach in protocol," said Paul. "But I agree. Hayes won't stand idly by until Tuesday. We need to get this done while we can."

When they arrived at the distillery, Julianna met Shane as he exited the Yukon. She passed him Gina's phone. "The mayor is getting antsy. He wants to know when he's going to see Evelyn."

"Thanks." Shane slung his rifle around to hang behind his back and replied to the text inquiry. *I'll return your daughter as soon as you return the guns, ammo, and supplies you stole from my house.*

Julianna watched as Shane typed. "He's not going to like having to renegotiate."

"I know, but I have to buy us some time so we can hold the elections. Plus, it's going to be hard to get by without those guns and supplies."

The mayor's text came quickly. Shane read it aloud for all to hear. "You're not going to nickel and dime me for the next week. I demand that you send her home right now!"

Or what? Shane replied. *Do you really want to call my bluff again? I'll remind you, that didn't end well the last time you tried it.*

Shane looked up at Bivens. "You should get going first thing in the morning. We can't keep this game up forever. Take Butterbean with you. Tell everyone the election will be at the old flea market on 74. Polls open at 8:00 AM and close at 4:00."

"I'll go at first light, but I need someone who can move if I get in trouble," Bivens replied.

Pastor Joel said, "I'll go with you. It will be a good chance to do some campaigning."

Elizabeth, Tonya, Maggie Farris, and Angela came out to meet the returning captives. Each hugged their respective husbands. All except Angela, that is.

"Where's Greg?" Her eyes were filled with concern.

"He was taken out of the cell where the rest of us were shortly after we were arrested," Paul replied.

"Where did they take him? Why would they do that?" She looked to Deputy Bivens for an explanation.

"I don't know," Bivens replied. "Butterbean said Greg wasn't listed as an inmate."

"What does that mean? They killed him?" Angela became progressively more upset.

"I don't think so," Bivens said. "It's more likely that they set him free."

"Why would they let Greg go before the rest of you?" She pleaded with her father for answers.

"I'm not sure, sweetheart." Paul hugged his daughter.

Shane looked at the phone. "The mayor is going to give us back the supplies."

"Have him drop them off tomorrow afternoon at the cabin," Paul said.

Shane looked at his father. "Someone is in the

cabin. I couldn't tell who, but I saw them walking around."

"Then we'll kill two birds with one stone. We'll get the supplies and clear out the squatters." Paul leaned on the vehicle. "We have a small window of relative immunity. We need to exploit it to the fullest extent."

Shane nodded and entered the reply.

CHAPTER 13

That which is crooked cannot be made straight: and that which is wanting cannot be numbered.

Ecclesiastes 1:15

Friday afternoon, Shane watched through the riflescope from the cover of the woods above the main cabin. Jackson Construction henchmen unloaded supplies from a box truck. Once finished, they closed the roll-down door, returned to the cab, and drove off. Julianna lay in the brush at the top of the hill next to him, also peering through her scope.

Shane picked up his walkie-talkie and spoke softly. "Dad, you and Fulton are clear to come pick up the packages. Once you finish loading up, Julianna, Bobby, and I will see who our uninvited guest is."

Paul's voice came over the radio. "Okay, we'll drop the goods at Dan's old hunting cabin and come back to pick you up. I don't want to take anything to the distillery. One of the packages could have a tracking device hidden inside."

"Roger that. Bobby, hold your position until Dad's team leaves with the food and guns. We'll flank both sides of the cabin, so our guest has nowhere to run." Shane looked over to the adjacent tree line where the big man kept watch from a different vantage point. He saw his head nod.

Shane watched quietly while his father and Fulton arrived at the property and collected the supplies. While they waited, he said to Julianna, "I appreciate you coming out here with us. I know it was difficult to leave Cole behind, but he's in good hands with my mom."

"Cole is the reason I'm doing this." She adjusted the butt of her rifle to be more firmly seated against her shoulder. "After he was abducted, my worldview changed drastically. Losing Will didn't help things either. I'm quickly coming around to the fact that the new normal requires a kill-or-be-killed mentality to survive."

"I'm sorry about that," he consoled.

"Unlike so many other things, I can't blame you for the world burning down." She turned briefly to hide the playful smile threatening to take control of her expression. Seriousness quickly returned. "I never really thanked you for helping to bring Cole home. His safety and wellbeing are your responsibility, but to your credit, you risked your life before you even knew he was your son. So, thank you for that."

"I only wish I had known sooner. Not that it's your fault that I didn't. I take full responsibility for being a jerk."

"I won't argue with that." Her tone was less accusatory than it had been during recent conversations. "Anyway, with Dan injured and Greg missing, our little compound is getting thin on shooters. It's time I stepped up to the plate, did my part to keep Cole as safe as possible."

"Have you given any more thought about telling Cole?"

She sighed. "When the time is right."

Shane knew he deserved no better, so he didn't push the subject.

"Get ready," Julianna pointed to the truck at the bottom of the hill. "They're leaving."

Shane picked up the radio. "Bobby, if our guest tries to run, let off one warning shot but then take him down if he doesn't stop. I want to give him a chance, but I can't risk this guy being a spy for Hayes and getting away. Let's work our way down the hill quietly."

Shane and Julianna began their descent. Each kept their rifles trained on the doors and windows of the main cabin. Shane saw the door open on the porch overlooking the driveway. He put his hand on Julianna's arm to stop her. Then, he looked to Bobby and held up his hand signaling for him to stop. Shane took aim and watched someone emerge from inside the house.

He yelled out. "Move a muscle and you'll be

gunned down before you can reach the door!"

The person looked over to Shane. It was Greg. "Shane, oh, man. Am I glad to see you!"

"I bet you are. Bobby, if he moves, kill him. Julianna and I are going inside to make sure he's alone."

"I got this." Bobby leveled his rifle in line with Greg's torso.

Shane led the way, taking his keys from his pocket when they arrived at the basement door. He and Julianna entered and proceeded to clear the house. Next, they came out onto the porch. "Face down on the ground!" Shane secured Greg's hands with zip ties. "Bobby, come on up."

Shane quizzed. "Tell us how you managed to get out of jail when everyone else was set to hang?"

Greg replied, "I went through SERE training when I was in the service. I saw my opportunity to escape and I took it. I got away. I figured I'd come back here and try to organize a rescue mission with you and Dan."

"You knew Dan and I wouldn't be here."

Greg relaxed, letting his head rest on the wooden deck of the covered porch. "I hoped you'd come back."

Shane patted him on the back. "Sounds like they didn't teach you much about putting together a good cover story in SERE school. I'm not buying it. You can tell me here and now, or we can take a trip down to Pastor Joel's confessional, in the basement of the guest house. You remember how bloody that got, don't you?"

"Angela will never forgive you if you do that to

me."

Julianna grabbed Greg by the mouth. "I'll never forgive him if he doesn't."

"You'll never forgive him anyway." Greg turned to face her.

She put her face closer to Greg's. "Who says I won't enjoy cutting you up myself? Angela and I aren't really that close, so I think I could live with her being angry with me. At least better than I could live with myself for letting a rat into the camp."

Bobby picked Greg up from the ground by the collar of his shirt and his belt. "I was Shane's bodyguard before the dollar died. I used to get paid to slap people around. I'll do the honors."

Greg seemed to quickly realize that Shane and his crew had forgone the good-cop-bad-cop routine in lieu of a much more frightening approach where they all acted as if they wanted a pound of flesh. "Okay, okay! Put me down. I'll tell you what happened."

Bobby let him go and Greg thumped on the floor. "Let's hear it."

"Ahhhh!" Greg yelped in pain as his face slammed against the floor.

With his mouth and nose bleeding he said, "It was obvious that you guys were on the losing side. You all don't stand a chance against an entire city and county full of corrupt politicians. It's not like they're bought off by the local organized crime bosses. They *are* the local organized crime bosses. At some point, when I was a drone pilot blowing up civilians alongside terrorists for the good of the country, I came to the realization that might makes right. It's how I learned to live with myself. It's how I went to sleep at night after a hard day's work of doing some pretty questionable stuff. You can't fight it. It's survival of the fittest."

"Don't confuse this situation with serving your country. I don't know what happened before, but this is on you." Shane said angrily, "You abandoned your wife, my sister, to save your own neck!"

"I was coming back for Angela, once all the toxic people were out of her life, and she could make a rational decision."

"Toxic people?" Shane squatted down next to the bound man. "You think my parents, the people who offered you a place to ride out the apocalypse, are toxic?"

Greg turned back toward the wooden deck. "I told you what you wanted to know."

"What are we going to do with him?" Bobby asked.

"Take him back, I guess. We'll throw him in the grain silo with Gina." Shane stood up. "We'll have to keep it from Angela for now. I'm not sure how she'll react. I'll tell her once the election is over with."

***

Back at Pawpaw's distillery, Shane rested on the narrow porch of the shotgun house. He checked Gina's phone regularly, anxiously awaiting the fury of Mayor Hayes when he, once again, had to delay the return of his daughter.

Cole came walking up from the trail which led to

the barn.

Julianna sat in the yard on an old fruit crate, one that had likely been used to transport Pawpaw's recipe in bygone years. "Where are you coming from?"

"Me and Scotty was trying to catch a mouse in the barn."

"You were supposed to stay with Mrs. Black, and it's *Scotty and I were trying to catch a mouse.* You don't want to sound like you're from the mountains."

The youngster looked confused. "But I am from the mountains."

"Nothing is wrong with being from the mountains, but you don't have to sound like it," she said.

Perplexed, the boy turned to Shane. "Are we ever gonna go fishing again?"

Shane wished he could bring his son home. "Yes. We'll go soon. But let's try to make the most of the time we have here. Don't you think it's fun camping in the big barn?"

The boy thought. "Well, I guess it's okay. But I'd rather be back at your house."

"Maybe we need to do some exploring. Let's go look for crawdads and newts in the creek."

"Okay!" Cole pepped up right away. "Mama, ain't you gonna come?"

"Mama, aren't you going to come. And no, mamas don't like newts and crawdads."

"But I ain't seen you all day. I mean, I aren't seen you all day." He held out his hand to take hers.

She seemed to melt at Cole's plea to join them.

She lifted herself from the fruit crate and followed her son. Cole walked between them, holding Julianna's hand on one side, and Shane's on the other.

"One big happy family," she said sarcastically.

Shane thrilled at the thought but knew Julianna would have none of it. Once at the creek, Shane lifted rocks while Cole scurried to trap newts with his small hands. Julianna kept her distance, but the three of them laughed together each time another of the small water lizards successfully freed himself from Cole's eager fingers.

Shane froze when he felt the phone vibrate in his pocket. He flipped the last rock for Cole and retrieved the device.

"He's mad?" Julianna asked.

"Not as mad as he's gonna be." Shane entered the text, letting the mayor know that they wouldn't be returning Evelyn until sunset the following day. He mentioned the fact that members of his group could potentially be moving about town on Friday and that if any of them were harassed, it would cost Evelyn her life.

Julianna looked over Shane's shoulder. She read the mayor's reply out loud. "You're still trying to hold illegal elections. This is where my patience ends. I'll bring in anyone caught participating in this treasonous activity."

Shane scowled. He typed back the reply. *Okay. I'll bring you your daughter… One piece at a time.*

Julianna looked on. "You kinda painted yourself in a corner with that one. How do you plan to pull off that bluff?"

Shane looked to make sure Cole was out of earshot. "I'll bring him a finger. I think that will buy us the time we need to have the election."

Her eyes narrowed. "You're not really going to…"

"An adult's pinky could look a lot like a twelve-year-old's index finger."

"Still," she looked at him apprehensively, "Who's going to volunteer their pinky for the sake of the elections?"

"After everything Greg has put us through, I think this small contribution is the least he can do."

"You think your dad is going to sign off on this?"

"I'll discuss it with him when I return."

"From where?"

"From delivering the finger to Mayor Hayes."

"It's too risky. You can't. Cole has already lost one father."

Shane handed her the phone. "Then if I get in a tight spot, you better be convincing."

"You're not going alone, are you?" She sounded concerned.

"I'll take Bobby. He's bailed me out of more than one scrape." He patted Cole on the head. "I'll see you later, buddy. I've got some business to attend to."

"Shane," Julianna called as he walked away.

"Yes?" He turned to face her.

After a brief pause, her eyes glanced up at his. "Be safe."

"I will." Shane set out upon his gruesome mission. After abducting a little girl from the safety of her own home, he felt sure that cutting off Greg's pinky would be a piece of cake.

***

Shane and Bobby marched up the stairs and past the roughneck security personnel guarding the mayor's big white house on Haywood Road. The two men at the door drew their weapons. One was the pale, towering Sylva PD officer who Bobby called Lurch.

"Where do you two think you're going?" asked Officer Hicks.

"We're here to see the mayor." Shane held a shoebox under his arm.

"Do you have an appointment?" Hicks pointed his gun at Shane's head.

"Tell him I brought his daughter back."

Hicks glanced at the shoe box, then up at Shane. He knocked on the door. "Boss, we need you outside."

Wallace Hayes opened the door, still dressed in his three-piece suit like a career gangster politician. "Shane Black. You've got some guts showing up here." His eyes glared with malice and abhorrence.

"I told you I'd bring her back, one piece at a time. And I told you not to test my resolve again." Shane handed the shoebox to the mayor.

"Are you mad?" The mayor ripped open the box. He unfurled a blood-soaked rag to reveal the human digit contained therein. He gasped in horror, fumbling, and nearly dropping the finger. He dropped to his knees to recover the dismembered pinky, thinking it to belong to his precious daughter. His face revealed the thoughts of agony going through his mind, imagining the anguish his sweet little girl must have endured. He looked up at Shane as if to plead for mercy on behalf of his only child. "Can it be reattached?"

Shane maintained a callous stare. "No—and neither can her head. Keep that in mind tomorrow."

The mayor looked broken. His lip quivered and he dropped his gaze like a dog recognizing the dominance of a stronger animal. "You won't have any more trouble from me."

Without speaking, Shane motioned to Bobby, turned and walked back down the stairs.

CHAPTER 14

I am not afraid of an army of lions led by a sheep; I am afraid of an army of sheep led by a lion.

Alexander the Great

Saturday afternoon, Shane sat in the middle of the lowered tailgate of his father's pickup truck, his rifle propped up on the edge. Bobby leaned against the right side of the tailgate, taking up more than his allotted space. This pushed Shane closer to Julianna, who sat on his left. The three of them guarded the parking lot of the old flea market. They watched people come and go. Most left immediately after casting their ballots. Others milled about, speculating whether Hayes would go peacefully after the results were in. Some arrived in vehicles, expending precious fuel resources to exercise their civic duty. Others walked, while still others came on horseback or bicycles.

Deputy Bivens, Butterbean, and ten more former law enforcement officers provided security at the entrance of the single polling station.

"I can't believe we pulled this off," Bobby said.

"Don't count your chickens just yet," Julianna warned.

"Why? What could go wrong at this point?" Bobby leaned further back as if basking in a hard-earned moment of relaxation.

Shane felt the phone in his pocket buzz. "I hope you didn't just jinx us with that comment."

"You don't believe in that stuff, do you?" Bobby laughed.

Shane looked at the text. "Five minutes ago, I would have said no. Now, I'm not so sure."

Julianna leaned against Shane's shoulder to read the text. "Please don't hurt Evelyn. Sheriff Hammer caught wind of the election. He's determined to shut it down. I can't get him to back down. He's probably headed your way. This has nothing to do with me. I'm doing the best thing I know to do by warning you. Please don't hurt my daughter."

She looked up at Shane. "Do you think he's sincere?"

Bobby answered for him. "He's sincere. I've never seen a man look so shattered as he did yesterday. I almost felt bad for him."

Shane nodded his concurrence. "Bobby is right. Hayes is telling us the truth. We need to warn the others and get ready for a showdown." He jumped from the back of the truck and led the way to the simple building.

Shane spoke with Bivens first, since he was running security. "Eric, I just got a message from Hayes. Hammer is on his way here to shut down the polls."

"I'll spread the word," replied the deputy. "Go tell your father and try to convince any of the citizens you know to join us. This could get ugly."

Julianna patted Shane on the shoulder. "I see Mr. Mercer and his son-in-law in that group over there. I'll see if any of them are willing to help."

Shane nodded, then he and Bobby went inside to find Paul and Pastor Joel. They were gathered around the coffee station with George Franz, James and Jimmy Teague, along with several other townspeople who were running for office. Shane quickly relayed the message he'd received from Hayes.

The circle of men grew quiet. Terrance Camp, who was running for city commissioner said, "We should shut down the poll. Clear out before he gets here."

Paul looked at his watch, then up at the others. "It's only 1:30. We need to keep the polls open until 4:00. Otherwise, the results will be challenged."

"The results won't matter if all the elected officials are dead!" argued Camp.

"Then you better aim steady and shoot straight." Jimmy Teague handed a rifle to Camp.

Camp studied the faces of his compatriots. He took the weapon reluctantly. "Fine. If no one else is interested in a common sense solution, I suppose I won't waste my breath arguing for one."

Brady Watkins, a weathered old mountain man running for county commissioner, stuck his hands in the top of his overalls. "We ain't got no means of retreat. River runs right behind this place, and it's runnin' too high and too fast to get across it without a raft or somethin'. If we fight, it's a fight to the death."

Paul looked at the other men. "Anyone who wants to leave, go ahead. No one will think any less of you. At least I won't."

"I'm not going anywhere," said Pastor Joel.

The men from the Teague family all acknowledged their willingness to fight. Soon, everyone present had thrown in his lot; everyone except Terrance Camp, that is. They all watched him. Shane waited to see if he would leave.

After looking around at the other men for a few more seconds, Camp said, "I'm in, too, I guess."

Shane patted him on the back for encouragement. "We'll get through this."

Eric Bivens walked up to the men in the group. "My men are going to take up positions outside. We've brought in some of the townspeople who are willing to take a stand with us also. I'm sending them inside. Hopefully, Hammer will back down when he sees how many of us there are and realizes that we're ready to fight. But if he doesn't, my men will fire first. If we're overrun, we'll need you folks to cover us until we get inside. From here, we have to hold the fort at all costs. We can't let them get inside. We don't have a back door to slip out if things get hot. This is do or die."

Paul stroked his beard. "It's a good plan, Eric. But I hate not having a backup plan for when things go wrong. In my life, I've seen some pretty well-laid plans go belly-up. Not that anyone else could have come up with anything better on such short notice, but holding the fort is a coin toss at best."

Eric let his hand rest on his holster. "It's the best I can come up with, considering it was cobbled together at the last minute. What do you suggest to improve our odds?"

Paul walked to the window. "I'd position some shooters across the street. We could put a couple snipers on top of those self-storage buildings. The roofs are relatively flat."

"We'd be splitting up our small force," said Bivens.

"Yes, but if Hammer wants to take on all of us, he'll have to split up his people," Paul replied.

"Okay." Bivens nodded. "I'll put my best shooters across the street. I'll also find out who the hunters are among the townspeople."

"We all hunt." James Teague pointed at his sons and grandsons.

"I can drop a buck from clear across the county," boasted Brady Watkins.

"Good," said Bivens. "You men, follow me."

After they had left, Julianna came in. "Hammer is in for a fight."

Shane hated to see her in danger. "That's what I'm afraid of. Why don't you head on back to the distillery?"

"No thanks. I told you how I feel about all of this."

Shane's brow dipped lower. "Then at least go with Bivens. You're a good shot. He can put you on the roof as a sniper."

"Where are you going to fight?"

"I'm going to stay here, with my dad."

"Are you trying to get rid of me?" she asked.

"What? No! Of course not!" He was caught off guard by the statement. "But if you're across the street and Hammer starts winning, at least you'd have the woods as a means of getting away. The people in here, we're not leaving until the last bullet is fired."

"Then neither am I. Wherever you're fighting, that's where I'll be." She looked him in the eyes for a moment, then quickly turned away. "And Bobby, your dad, Pastor Joel. I don't want to be sent off by myself into the forest."

Shane had no time to decipher Julianna's tangled sub-text. He couldn't allow himself to be distracted by some desire which would likely never be fulfilled. "Okay, let's get into position. Bobby and I are both running 5.56. We'll set up by the window on the left with extra ammo. You can stay with us."

"Shouldn't we knock the glass out of the window? Won't it be less of a problem if it's already gone before the shooting starts?" asked Julianna.

Shane looked to his father. "What do you think?"

"I'd hate to bust up this fellow's shop for no reason. But if the range goes hot, Julianna is right. Bobby, can you take care of that for us?"

"Yes, sir," said the towering man. "Do you want me to take out all the windows?"

Paul nodded. "I think that would be best. Try as hard as you can to get the glass to land outside. We don't want to be crawling around on it when the fun starts."

Shane and Julianna followed Bobby around with a trash can, broom, and dustpan, sweeping up the stray shards which ended up on the inside of the building.

Butterbean's voice came over Shane's radio. "I see Jackson County Sheriff's Department vehicles coming this way."

"How many?" Shane asked.

"I'd say all of them," the deputy replied.

Shane grimaced. "For those of us who've never worked for any of the local departments, can you give us an approximation?"

"At least thirty vehicles." Butterbean's voice went higher, evidencing his stress level.

"Okay, thanks." Shane motioned to the people in the large room. "Everyone, this is it. Let's get ready."

Paul walked up to the window where Shane, Bobby, and Julianna were stationed. "Hang on to my rifle. I'm going to try taking Hammer down when he gets here."

Shane took the weapon and leaned it against the wall. "You're going out there unarmed?"

"I have my pistol, but this is about trying to avoid bloodshed. I don't want to go out there with a stance which will provoke violence."

Deep creases ran across Shane's forehead. "If he's attempting to break up a populist movement trying to remove him from office, we may be well past that point."

Paul didn't seem naive to the risk. "I have to try. If even one trigger ends up being pulled, a lot of people are going to die."

"I'll walk out there with you." Shane leaned his rifle against the wall.

Paul took the gun and handed it back to Shane. "You just cover me."

A phalanx of patrol vehicles sped into the parking lot, turning at an angle to face the building, and stopping short. The doors flew open on all sides of the vehicles and men with guns poured out, taking cover behind the doors. Some of the men wore Jackson County Sheriff's uniforms, while an even larger number of the men wore hunting clothes or personal tactical gear. Shane shook his head. "Looks like Hammer has recently deputized some of the county's more questionable residents."

Julianna took aim. "Once he hired Jacob Van Burren as a deputy, I guess the word got out that any thug could get a badge and a gun."

Sheriff Hammer stood behind the passenger's door of the center vehicle, an Expedition. Over the intercom, he called out to the people inside the building. "This is an unlawful assembly. I demand that you exit the building with your hands up. Anything other than immediate and total compliance will be met with deadly force."

Paul looked at Shane and smiled. "This is it."

"Be careful!" said Shane.

"I will." Paul put his hands up and walked out the door.

Hammer's voice yelled over the intercom. "Paul

Black. Stop where you are and lie face down on the ground."

"I can't do that, Harvey. I'm here to talk."

"You're wearing a pistol. You're a threat to myself and my officers. Face down, on the ground."

"This is not an unlawful assembly. These people are here to exercise their most basic constitutional rights. We're protected under the 1st Amendment to peaceably assemble and under the 2nd to be armed. Any attempt to interfere with this lawful assembly will be construed as treason, and we will defend our rights with force if necessary." Paul kept his hands up but his voice loud.

POW! A shot rang out from behind Hammer's door. Paul toppled forward. Shane's skin went cold, his heart stopped, his mind raced to understand what had just happened.

CHAPTER 15

Is life so dear, or peace so sweet, as to be purchased at the price of chains and slavery? Forbid it, Almighty God! I know not what course others may take, but as for me, give me liberty or give me death!

Patrick Henry

    Shane quickly closed his gaping jaw and turned to Julianna. "Cover me!" He motioned for Bobby. "We have to bring my dad inside!"
    Bobby nodded and followed Shane out the door. Both sides of the line erupted in gunfire. Rifles, shotguns, and pistols exploded in a deadly barrage of ballistic projectiles. Shane tucked low, slid into the gravel next to his father and helped him up.

Bobby grabbed the other side. The two of them ran beneath a gauntlet of annihilation, dragging the wounded man between them.

Once inside the building, Shane said, "Dad, hang on!" He looked at the blood oozing out of his father's chest.

Paul gasped in pain. "Kill Hammer. Worry about me later. If he gets inside, we're all dead anyway."

"Come on, Shane." Bobby gently coaxed him away from the bleeding man. "We need you in the fight."

Shane hesitated to leave his father's side.

"Go!" Paul pointed.

Shane tore his gaze from his injured father. He pressed the butt of his weapon against his shoulder. He looked out the window to see Hammer's men rolling the patrol cars closer to the building while using the vehicles for shields. Gunfire peppered the concrete blocks near his head. Bits of debris hit the side of his face as he ducked behind the wall. Julianna held her weapon over the edge of the window and fired blindly.

Shane pointed to Bobby. "Help her put down cover fire. I'm going to see if I can get a shot out the door."

Bobby complied. "You better hurry. They're gonna be on top of us in about one minute."

Shane rolled over to the doorway on his stomach. He had a clear shot, but his only target was the feet of the men behind the vehicles. Shane opened fire. He directed rounds toward one set of ankles, then the next. A couple of the men fell to the ground, providing headshots which Shane quickly seized upon. Others took refuge inside the patrol cars. Shane felt proud of the six or seven hostiles he'd been able to take out of the fight by killing or injuring.

Then, as quickly as his reign of terror had begun, it was over. Click! His magazine was empty. He looked to his left. "Pastor Joel, keep firing!"

The pastor, Fulton Farris, and Terrance Camp all shot wildly while Shane changed magazines. Shane rolled back to the opening and searched for targets. It was too late. Hammer's men had evidently grown wise to his ploy and were now all inside the vehicles. "They're coming this way!"

Shane watched the vehicles creep closer to the building while Hammer and his men bombarded the flea market building with lead and fire. He knew targeting the tires of the vehicles would do nothing to stop them. They could roll on rims for the next twenty feet, bringing the patrol cars right up to the door.

George Franz shot several rounds from the adjacent window, then ducked behind the cover of the concrete wall. "This would be a good time to call in the cavalry."

Shane nodded and pressed the talk key on his radio. "Eric, light 'em up."

"Okay, have your people take cover and hold their fire," he replied.

"Cease fire! Cease fire! Get down! Take cover!" yelled Shane. He watched as Julianna and Bobby got as low to the floor as possible. Shane listened to the fusillade of guns thundering on the other side of the wall. He could hear the moans of agony coming from Hammer's men who'd been caught off guard by the ambush.

During the respite, Shane tore off his flannel shirt and balled it up as he crawled to his father's side. He pressed it against the wound. "Keep pressure on this."

Paul nodded shallowly. "Thank you." His eyes were half-open.

Bivens' voice came over the radio. "Shane, I need your team back in the fight. They are on to us and coming this way. Be aware of what's behind your targets. This is a bad situation."

Shane looked around at the other people in the room. "Did everybody get that?"

All nodded.

"Good, let's cut Hammer down!" Shane turned his attention to his father. "I'll be right back."

"Do what you have to do, son."

Shane took up his position in the doorway and began shooting once again. He killed three more of Hammer's men before the enemy force realized they were being picked off from both sides.

Hammer's voice came over the intercom of one of the cars. "Circle the vehicles. They're all around us!"

"We can't let them do that!" Shane shouted. "We need to get out there and kill Hammer before he gets organized."

"I'm with you," said Bobby.

Shane nodded. "George, you and Julianna lay down some heavy cover fire. The rest of us will hit them while they are still on the run."

Camp looked nervous. "We're going out there?"

Shane had no time to babysit. He pressed the talk key. "Bivens, we're going to make a run at them. Tell your men to watch out for us."

"Roger that!"

Shane motioned for the pastor, Bobby, and the others to line up at the door behind him. "Go!" Shane led his team to the first vehicle where they cut down all of Hammer's men. They took cover behind that patrol car and regrouped. "We'll do the same thing to the next car." Shane pointed to their next target. He looked back to the window where Julianna was standing with her rifle ready. He nodded to her and pointed in the direction he would lead his team. She and George Franz unleashed a second volley of cover fire while Shane tucked low and initiated the assault on the next vehicle.

This time, Hammer's men popped up from a nearby vehicle and countered the attack. Shane felt immersed in danger. Bullets flew and cartridges discharged all around him. He looked for targets and fired as quickly as he could but wasn't sure where his teammates were. The confusion was overwhelming, but he kept fighting. He had no other choice.

Shane saw Fulton Farris fall to the ground on his left. Then, Terrance Camp dropped his weapon and grabbed his arm. Shane didn't know what to do.

Julianna yelled from somewhere. It took Shane a moment to orient his directions, to even tell where her voice was coming from.

"Shane, get out of there! Come back!" she cried.

Shane followed the sound, motioning for Bobby, Pastor Joel, and the others to come after him.

Julianna and George continued to provide covering fire for the retreat. Shane collapsed to the floor, taking a second to regain his bearings. He examined Bobby and Pastor Joel but saw no bullet wounds.

Terrance Camp squealed in torture. "My arm! My arm!"

Shane glanced around the side of the door to see Fulton Farris lying on the gravel, his face turned toward the building. His eyes were open, but his expression was blank. Shane pressed the talk key once more. "Eric, we're getting eaten alive over here."

"I'm pressing toward you, but it looks like they're going to breach your entrance. You better find somewhere to hole up inside."

Shane didn't want to hear that. He looked around the room but saw nothing that would stop a bullet. He signaled to Bobby. "Take my dad out the back door. Lay prone on the riverbank and hold the line. If we lose that position, we'll have nowhere left to run."

Bobby nodded and scooped Paul up off the ground. Shane fired at the approaching men, but they just kept coming. He looked at Julianna. "You, too. Get Terrance Camp out of here. George, go with them."

Shane kept firing as did Pastor Joel and the others. Nevertheless, Hammer's men continued to gain ground. Shane waited until the last minute, killing two more who were only feet away from coming in the door. "Okay, everybody out!" he shouted. Shane changed his magazine and walked backward, ushering the others out the back door, and letting off his final cannonade from the AR-15.

Once outside, Shane dashed to the riverbank. "Everyone, reload and get in a prone position facing the back door. We'll pick them off as they come out. This is our Alamo. Hold it with your lives."

Soon, Hammer's men came rushing through the door like a swarm of hornets. They emerged with guns blazing. Shane and the others returned fire as quickly as they could. He heard Pastor Joel yelp in pain. His mind sped up and time slowed down. Fervently, he strained to make his rifle fire faster, but he could not. In the space between the cycling of the weapon, Shane thought of one thing. He wished he'd done more to convince Julianna to get out of there before the inevitable slaughter.

Suddenly, Shane's bolt snapped open. His magazine was empty again. Before he could change his mags, he listened to Bobby's and Julianna's weapons both mimic his own. Shane quickly drew his pistol, hoping he could give the others enough time to reload. He ripped through round after round. From the corner of his eye, he saw Julianna and Bobby slap the bolt releases of their AR-15s.

"Hold your fire!" shouted a familiar voice. Shane watched the remaining three ruffians drop to the ground, inches from his face.

"I'm coming out!" called the voice. Eric Bivens walked through the door and lowered his weapon.

Shane looked at Julianna who was breathing heavily. He glanced at his friend, Bobby, who likewise was gasping for air. Shane nodded to them both, as each seemed unsure whether to believe that the nightmare was truly over.

Two other former deputies walked through the door behind Eric. "Do you have any wounded?"

Shane instantly remembered his father's perilous condition. "My dad!" He pointed down the embankment, near the water where Bobby had placed the man, as far from harm's way as possible.

"Pastor Joel, also." Julianna got up from her position to check on the pastor.

Terrance Camp spoke for himself. "I was shot in the arm! I'm bleeding badly!"

Bivens walked toward Paul. He addressed Shane and Bobby. "Get him back to your compound. My sister is a nurse practitioner. I'll go pick her up and bring her over. She can get him stabilized and will probably know a doctor who can help us."

"Can't we take him to the hospital? I know they're short staffed and low on supplies, but it has to be better than our house," Shane argued.

Eric shook his head. "We ended this so fast because Hammer took off with about twenty guys. He's still out there. If he decides to make a second strike the hospital will be the first place he goes."

Pastor Joel was up and walking. He'd been hit in the shoulder, so Julianna followed him, carrying his rifle. She said, "The farm will be as much at risk as anywhere."

"I don't think so," said Bivens. "Only one avenue of approach. I'll send my men over there as well as the Teagues. We'll use the Blacks' place for our forward operating base until this thing is settled."

Shane acquiesced to Eric Bivens' suggestion. "Okay. Get going. We'll try to have him cleaned up by the time you arrive with your sister."

Bobby helped to take Paul to the truck where they laid him gently in the back seat. "Do you want me to drive?"

Shane put his hand on his friend's shoulder. "I need you to do something more important."

"Anything, just name it," replied the big man.

"Can you ride out to Murphy? I need you to bring my mother and sister home. If these are his final moments, they'll want to say goodbye."

Bobby lowered his gaze. "I'll do it. What about the others? Should I tell them to come back as well?"

"Yeah, but get Mom and Angela back as quickly as you can." Shane grieved as he beheld the frail man who'd always been a pillar of strength. Paul was unconscious and his breathing was faint.

"Why don't I drive? You can ride in the back with your father," offered Julianna.

"Okay, thanks." Shane put his weapons in the floorboard and gently placed his father's head in his lap.

Julianna looked to Pastor Joel. "Do you need help getting in the truck?"

"I can manage." The pastor got in and pulled the door closed with his good hand. Once inside, he began praying. Not for himself, but for Paul and the others who had been injured during the skirmish.

CHAPTER 16

Greater love hath no man than this, that a man lay down his life for his friends.

John 15:13

Late Saturday evening, Shane, Angela, and Tonya sat around the bed in the basement guestroom of the main cabin. Doctor Ackers checked Paul's pulse. He offered an anemic smile and stood up. "I'll leave you all to visit for a while."

Shane didn't dare ask how his father was doing. Everyone seemed to know, but no one acknowledged the presence of the death angel hovering like a dark cloud in the room.

A delicate knock came to the door. Shane turned to see Julianna standing in the entrance of the room. She spoke just above a whisper. "Eric Bivens is here. He wanted to know if he could see Paul, only for a minute."

Paul's eyes opened. He labored to lift his arm and open his lips. "Send him in."

"Sure." She smiled pleasantly and left the room.

Minutes later, Eric walked in. He stood next to Shane. "I wanted to give you the news myself."

Paul's voice was feeble. "Let's hear it."

"We tallied the votes. You're the new sheriff, Paul." Bivens handed the man a gold star badge. "This is just a deputy's badge, but we'll get the real one from Hammer soon enough."

He grinned and clutched the emblem in his weak hand. "Thank you. What about Pastor Joel?"

"Jimmy Teague secured the majority of the ballots in the mayoral race."

"Jimmy is a good man," Paul replied.

"Yes, sir; a very good man. Much better than what we had."

Paul cracked a wider smile. "A rabid polecat would be better than what we had."

"Yes, sir. Indeed, he would be." Eric's smile showed his remorse over the situation.

Paul closed his eyes as if tired from the news. Moments later, he opened them once more. "Eric?"

"Yes, sir?"

Paul held out the badge to Bivens, placing it in his palm. "I'm appointing you acting sheriff."

"Thank you, sir." Eric's lip quivered. "But you'll be up and about in no time."

Paul let his face relax and gave a gentle nod. "Even so, you look after things for me in the time being."

"I will, sir." Eric lifted his hand slightly to bid farewell to Shane, Angela, Tonya, and Paul. He excused himself from the room, leaving the family alone once more.

Angela put her head on her father's chest. "I'm sorry, Daddy."

"For what, sweetheart?" He patted her gently.

"For Greg. For what he did. It's his fault. He caused all of this." She dried her eyes with her shirt sleeve. "If I hadn't brought him home, none of this would have happened."

"Oh, baby," Paul said calmly. "You didn't know. You've been hurt by him more than any of us. Please don't blame yourself." He looked to Shane. "What did y'all do with him anyway?"

"Eric has Butterbean watching him. As soon as we take control of the municipal building and the jail, we'll lock him up for involvement in a criminal organization."

"What about Hayes' wife and daughter?"

Shane put his hand on his father's. "I gave Gina the keys to the Yukon. I told her she could do whatever she wanted. I expect she'll go back to Wallace Hayes. She doesn't strike me as a fast learner."

"Too, bad," Paul closed his eyes. "For the little girl, I mean."

Shane remembered the spunky pre-teen fondly. "Yeah. That one is as smart as a whip."

Tonya bent over to kiss her husband. "I love you, Paul."

He took her hand and held it tenderly. "And I love you, more than words can describe." His face was soft, happy, and content.

Paul's eyelids rose slightly to gaze at Shane. "You'll look after your mother and your sister for me."

"Of course, I will." Shane felt the knot in his throat.

"I'm proud of you, son. You came back home with your whole heart. It's all I ever wanted for you." Paul Black closed his eyes for the last time.

***

Shane eyed the pastor's sling after the memorial service Sunday afternoon. "Thank you, Pastor Joel. It was a beautiful eulogy you gave for Fulton and my father."

"Paul might have been the best man I ever knew." The pastor's voice cracked. He'd held his composure through the funeral, but it seemed he needed his time to mourn. "If you'll excuse me."

"Sure." Shane watched him walk away, then turned his attention back to the growing creek-side cemetery.

Julianna stood next to Cole, pressing his head against her leg. She gazed at Paul's grave. She knelt down beside her young son and spoke softly. "Cole, I need to tell you something. It's important, and I should have told you long ago."

"Okay." The boy seemed unaware of the life-altering information he was about to receive.

"Paul was your grandpa."

Cole's face showed his bemusement. He glanced

at Shane.

Julianna took a deep breath. "Before I married daddy, Shane and I were together. We were boyfriend and girlfriend. We were together in a way that the Bible says people shouldn't be unless they're married; the kind of way that makes a baby. That's when you were made."

Cole's young mind seemed to be wrestling with what he was being told. He looked at his mother, then to Shane, then to Will's grave. After a few moments of contemplation, he looked at his mother. "It was a sin, you and Shane being together like that?"

She looked to the ground. "Yes, it was."

"I'm a sin?" he asked.

Instantly, she looked back up. "No, baby! You are a miracle, a precious gift from God. You didn't do anything wrong."

Cole looked to Shane as if seeking confirmation of his mother's statement.

Shane bit his lip and knelt beside his son. "You're my special blessing. I'm sorry we didn't do things the right way, but you are good. Your mother loves you, I love you, and God loves you."

Cole stared up innocently. "Are you going to marry Shane?"

"No, baby. I'm not going to marry Shane."

"Doesn't God want you to? So it wouldn't be a sin for making me?"

"God doesn't..." She sighed, seemed to search for a response. "Shane and I sinned against God. Getting married now wouldn't change that. And nothing we do will change what a wonderful boy you are."

"You don't love Shane?"

"I . . . I don't trust Shane. He left me—before."

Cole looked at Shane. "Are you going to leave again?"

Shane shook his head and hugged the boy. He held him tight so he wouldn't see the tears streaming down his face. "No, son. I'm never going to leave again. I promise."

Cole looked at Julianna. "What am I supposed to call Shane? Daddy?"

She shook her head. "Will is your daddy. Even though you weren't his biological son, he loved you more than life itself. Nothing will ever change that. You can keep on calling him Shane for now. Later on, if you decide you want to call him something else—that will be up to you."

Cole pulled away from Shane and looked him in his eyes. Shane quickly dried his cheeks.

Cole asked, "What else could I call you?"

Shane lifted his shoulders. "You could call me father or papa, but it's like your mom said, it's up to you."

"Okay." The boy examined him as if seeing him in a new light. "I'm going to have to think about it for a while."

"That will be just fine." Shane hugged him once more.

***

In the days that followed, the townspeople supported the newly elected officials. A grand procession was made down Main Street where the freshly chosen city and county administrators were sworn in with great pomp and celebration. The gathering also acted as a show of force. While Shane saw no pitchforks or torches, everyone old enough to pull a trigger seemed to have at least one weapon. Most of the citizens carried long guns and more than half wore pistols at their sides as well.

Many of the townsfolks thanked Shane for his role in bringing down the corrupt politicians connected to the Jackson Political Action Committee. Most offered their condolences for Paul and remembered his sacrifice in ridding the county of Jack PAC.

Life at the Black compound eventually fell into a routine. Security shifts were scheduled. The garden needed tending. Wood had to be cut and split. Chickens required feeding. Shane bartered with George Franz to purchase a pair of goats for some supplies. Everyone worked together to get things done. Those with specialized skills focused on what they did best.

Since they lived close by, the Franzs and the Teagues attended Sunday worship services with the residents of the Black compound and a generous potluck lunch was held each week after church.

Things were by no means back to normal, but the folks of Jackson County North Carolina, and especially those living at the Blacks' compound, fared far better than those in other parts of the country.

CHAPTER 17

Train up a child in the way he should go: and when he is old, he will not depart from it.

Proverbs 22:6

May 1st, three weeks after Paul Black's memorial service.

Early Monday morning, Shane went through the rows of the garden on his hands and knees. He used a piece of old cardboard to keep from getting dirt all over his pants. Cole trailed behind him inspecting his work. "Are those weeds?"

"No, they're peas, but they're too thick. I have to thin them out."

"What are you going to do with them?"

"Just leave them on the side of the garden, I guess."

"Could we feed them to the goats?"

"Sure. That's a very resourceful idea. Why don't you run up to the house and get a bucket? We'll use it to take the weeds and the vegetables I thin out to the goats."

"Goats eat weeds?" The young boy seemed surprised by the suggestion.

"Goats will eat anything they can fit in their mouth."

Cole appeared to ponder his newly gleaned knowledge as he made his way up the hill to the house.

Shane continued his task. Minutes later, he looked up to see if Cole was coming back. Instead, he saw two figures approaching from the gravel drive. Shane dusted off his hands and stood up to get a better look at the visitors. He quickly recognized the men as his neighbors, James Teague and his son, the mayor, Jimmy Teague. "Mr. Teague, Mr. Mayor." Shane extended his hand when the men came closer.

"Good morning." James shook his hand then retrieved a small plastic bag from his top overalls pocket. He handed it to Shane.

Shane took it and examined the contents. "Wow! Those are big corn kernels."

"It's flour corn. The old folks around here used to call it bread corn," said the elderly man. "We appreciate them seeds you brought us. Our garden would have been mighty poorly if we'd had nothing but the seeds we saved from last year."

"I can't take credit for it. My dad was the one who stockpiled the seeds." Shane looked his garden plot over. "I suppose I could plow a few more rows near the bottom of the garden."

The old man shook his head. "Best plow you another field. Put it up near the front of your property. The wind will blow pollen from the corn you've already planted to your bread corn and vice versa. You'll wind up with corn so sorry the chickens won't peck it."

"Oh, thanks for telling me. I didn't know."

"Yep. I had some leftover sweet corn seeds from last year. We fixed a separate plot to keep it away from the field corn. It's hybrid, so this will be the last of it. I'll bring you a few ears when it comes in."

"I appreciate that." Shane looked at Jimmy. "How are things with the city?"

"Still ain't seen hide nor hair of Hammer; Wallace Hayes neither. We don't have the manpower or the resources to hunt them down. The men assisting Sheriff Bivens are essentially volunteers, which means they work two days a week. We simply don't have a way to compensate them. Some of the townspeople bring in what they can spare to feed the deputies. But they need more than a dozen eggs or a bag of venison jerky to get by."

"I could volunteer for a day or two a week, Bobby would probably come with me. Dan is mending well. I'm sure he would also."

"I'll tell Eric. I'm sure he'd appreciate the help." Jimmy Teague laughed at Cole hauling the big five-gallon bucket. "That thing is almost as big as you."

"I can carry it," boasted the lad.

"I see that." Jimmy smiled and turned back to Shane. "Our most immediate need is fuel. If we can't keep the patrol vehicles gassed up, the shortage of manpower won't matter."

"Sorry, we don't have any to spare." Shane put his arm on the shoulder of his son who stood at his side.

"Marathon Petroleum had a refinery up in Kentucky. Catlettsburg, it's about six hours from here," said Jimmy.

"Are they still operational?" asked Shane.

"No one is answering the phones, so officially, probably not. If they were, I'm sure the federal government would have nationalized it. But gasoline is about the most precious commodity in the country. A refinery is the modern equivalent of a gold mine. I can't imagine the people living nearby, especially the ones who used to work at the refinery, letting such a resource sit idle."

Shane dangled the plastic baggy of corn seed. "Think we can convince them that these are magic corn seeds that will grow all the way to the clouds?"

"Probably not," chuckled Jimmy. "Your dad was a wise man. I know he took certain precautions against the economic collapse. He tried to talk to me about it more than once. I wish I had listened more closely and heeded his advice. I could never conceive we'd go through such a catastrophic upheaval. Your father, however, seemed to have watched the whole thing go down in flames through his crystal ball."

Shane remembered all the things Paul had taught him over the years. "It was no crystal ball. Just a careful observation of history. Nothing about the death of the dollar was particularly noteworthy from a historical standpoint. It's what always happens. The only reason we think of it as such an incredible event is because this time, it happened to us."

Jimmy nodded. "Your dad always said that gold was the currency the world would turn to when fiat money failed. I expect he followed his own advice. I hate to ask this of you, but would you happen to have any resources you could allocate toward securing fuel to keep things running a while longer?"

Shane thought about what was being asked of him. This wasn't Wallace Hayes strong-arming him for his own personal gain, this was his friends and neighbors. "Whatever my father put aside belongs to my mother. So that would be something I'd have to speak to her about."

"Sure, I understand," said the mayor.

Shane felt bad about turning him down. "But I might have some resources of my own that could help. How much do you think it would take?"

Jimmy looked at his father. "I don't have the slightest idea. But I would imagine if the Catlettsburg refinery is producing gasoline, gold will be the thing they are selling it for. At some point, we may be able to produce enough of something to barter, but we're a long way off right now."

"How would you transport the fuel?" asked Shane. "Even if they are producing, they may not be willing to accept the risk to move the product. According to the latest reports on NPR, the highways are a good place to die."

"Roads that go through major cities are the most dangerous," said the mayor. "Catlettsburg is due north. If you skirt around Asheville, you can get there without going through a town with more than five stoplights. We could use one of the water tankers from the fire department. The big one holds 5,000 gallons."

"A big red truck with lights on the top." Shane grinned. "It's not exactly an inconspicuous way to travel."

"Maybe not," said the eldest Teague. "But it don't say gasoline on the side of the truck neither."

"Point taken," Shane conceded. He turned to the new mayor. "Who's going to make the run?"

Jimmy looked at his father. "My brother, Johnny, for one. He knows the roads up through there. Eric will probably go also."

"Two people?" Shane's brow wrinkled. "Not having to go through a big city like Atlanta or Nashville reduces the risk, but Wallace Hayes taught us that mountain folk can be just as ornery as city people when they get greedy or desperate."

The mayor tightened his jaw. "Like I said, we're short staffed, what with not being able to pay folks and all."

"It would be good if you had at least a security team to escort the payload. I packed up and left when things first started melting down. Bobby and I survived that trip by the skin of our teeth." Shane recalled the horrific events of that day. He bowed his head. "My girlfriend wasn't as fortunate." Shane brought his eyes back up to Jimmy's. "It's ten times worse out there now. It's like a bad zombie movie on the roads these days."

"So are you volunteering to go?" the mayor asked.

Shane looked down at his son. Cole looked up at him, as if expecting him to step up to the plate. Shane cast his gaze back toward his cabin, his fortress of safety. "I don't know, Jimmy. It's not a very solid plan."

"Sylva and the rest of Jackson County is going to be like a bad zombie movie if we can't put gas in our patrol cars." Jimmy's expression grew grim. "Without a show of force to the would-be vandal hordes, our little town is going to look like an open buffet. I'm not saying it has to be you, or even that it should be you, but someone is going to have to try."

Shane looked over the property. "If I put up the capital for the trip, can I get some kind of receipt? Something like prepayment for ever how many years' worth of taxes my investment is worth?"

Jimmy smiled. "I think I can talk to some folks at the county and make that happen. When the dollar finally hit bottom, I think gold was around $10,000. Your tax can't be more than a couple grand a year. An ounce of gold should pre-pay you out for about five years. How much do you think you'd be willing to part with?"

"If you can get me a receipt that states I'm paid in full, I'll pay up the next fifty years."

James whistled and looked at his son. "Ten

ounces of gold! I wish I'd had the sense to trade in that worthless stack of bills for real money."

Jimmy nodded. "It will be much appreciated. Even so, it's not going to fill up a 5,000-gallon tanker. Let's say they value the gold at $10,000 an ounce. Gas was close to $100 a gallon the last time it was readily available."

"Because it was being priced in a worthless currency unit," Shane countered. "OPEC is settling oil for gold. The last quote I heard was one one-hundredth of an ounce per barrel. 42 gallons in a barrel. So, an ounce should buy 4200 gallons of crude on the international market. Gasoline runs anywhere from 2-to-3 times the cost of unrefined oil. Any way you slice it, we should be able to get that tanker filled for less than five ounces."

"Except you're leaving out one important variable," said the old man.

"What's that?" Shane inquired.

"We ain't in the international market. We're livin' in one of them horror picture shows you boys keep bringin' up."

Shane knew the elder Teague's point was a valid one. "Maybe so, but there's a limit to how far I'm going to let them rake us over the coals in this deal. I'll tell them that we'll walk away if we can't get it filled for ten ounces. We'll say that we know of a refinery down in Louisiana that will fill it for half that amount."

Jimmy grinned slyly. "So, let me get this straight. Not only are you going, but you'll also be heading up negotiations for us as well?"

Shane grimaced. "I suppose I have to look after

my investment."

CHAPTER 18

A man that hath friends must shew himself friendly: and there is a friend that sticketh closer than a brother.

Proverbs 18:24

After lunch Monday afternoon Shane leaned against the doorframe of Bobby's trailer. "I hate to put you on the spot like this. If you don't want to do it, I understand. I can try to find somebody else. Dan would probably go, but his leg still hurts him when he sits for a long time. Pastor Joel would come if I needed him to, but that long drive won't help his shoulder. I suppose it comes down to you being the only person not nursing a bullet wound."

"Yet." Bobby tied his bootlaces getting ready for his shift guarding the entrance gate.

Shane set his mouth in a straight line. "Yet." He felt terrible for dumping such a perilous mission in his friend's lap.

Bobby's stern expression cracked like a thin sheet of ice under the pressure of a dump truck. A grin broke out and he looked up at Shane. "I'm just messing with you. Of course I'll go. I wouldn't miss it for the world."

"Thank you." Shane was less enthusiastic but felt better about having the huge fellow along for the ride. "It means a lot to me." Shane left Bobby to finish getting ready. He walked across the property and up the hill to the main cabin. He entered the garage and began putting together a list of items which he might need for the trip.

"What'cha doing?" Julianna stood in the doorway; her hands pushed down into the pockets of her jeans.

He glanced at her, then continued filling a pack with MREs. "Oh, nothing much. Just getting some things organized."

"Organized, huh?" Her face showed that she already knew the nature of his task. "Organized for a trip?"

Shane felt perturbed at having to explain an errand he'd hoped to keep under the radar. "Just running up to Kentucky for the day tomorrow. No big deal."

"For what?" She continued to dig.

Shane stopped what he was doing. He stood erect with his hands on his hips. "Fuel. How did you hear about it anyway?"

"Cole came to me crying. He said you were a liar

and that you were leaving again."

Shane's face contorted into a wad of regret. He looked at the concrete floor of the garage. "I didn't think he was listening. Did you tell him I was coming back?"

"I didn't tell him anything." Julianna approached the pack Shane had been loading and inspected the contents. "No one bothered to fill me in, so I really didn't have any information with which to enlighten him."

Shane tried not to let himself be bothered by her nosing through his stuff. "I'll talk to him about it. You don't owe me anything, but I'd appreciate it if you'd help me out when you can."

Julianna abandoned her interest in the backpack. "How so?"

"With Cole." Shane considered his words. He knew it was a subject on which he must tread carefully. "He still calls me Shane, which is fine. But I feel like he trusts me less now than before he knew I was his father."

"You mean before he knew that you left us." She crossed her arms. "What exactly do you think I could do to rectify that issue?"

Shane glanced over at the ammo boxes, wanting to get on with loading the magazines for tomorrow's trip. "I don't know. Maybe say something nice about me once in a while. Or at least don't keep constantly reminding him of my shortfall, like you do me."

"Like I do you." Her face snapped into a venomous glare. "You brought up the subject of why your son doesn't trust you. I simply suggested that you take your actions into consideration. I'll have you know that I never say anything about you to Cole. I'm beyond insulted to have you insinuate that I do.

"And if you want me to vouch for your character, tell him that you've changed, that you'd never do anything like that again, you'll have to prove it to me first. I'm not going to lie to my son for you, just so he can call you papa, or father, or whatever title you're hoping for.

"Cole's wellbeing is my highest priority, not your warm-fuzzy feelings from showing up and playing dad because your world came crashing down and there's nothing better to do."

Shane instantaneously wished he'd looked before he stepped into the steaming pile of manure which was all over his shoe. "It wasn't like that. What I did was wrong, but if I had known about Cole…"

She put her hand up, interrupting his defense. "I don't want to hear it."

Julianna dismissed herself from the conversation and walked to the door. She turned before exiting the garage. "And by the way, I'm coming with you tomorrow."

"What?" Shane felt completely caught off guard by this announcement. "You can't come."

"Why? Because I'm a girl?"

"Yes, I mean, no." Shane couldn't believe he even needed to have this conversation. "Because you're a mother. Cole's mother, to be more specific. He needs you. This is a dangerous trip."

"This is a dangerous world." Her eyes showed her determination. "If you guys don't succeed, if our community doesn't get gas and the sheriff's department can't maintain that thin blue line..." She shook her head as if considering every conceivable atrocity.

Shane finished her sentence. "I know, it will be like the zombie apocalypse."

"No." Fear of an unfathomable future glistened in her eyes. "Far worse than that. It will be like Detroit, Atlanta, New York, LA. People are starving to death. The radio said all of those cities have had reports of cannibalism. They're eating each other to stay alive."

Shane saw the distress on her face. "That won't happen here. We have plenty of food stored to get us through until the garden starts producing. We even have enough to get us through a couple of bad years."

"Yeah, and when the monsters who have survived by feeding on their fellow human beings figure that out, where do you think they're going to come? They won't be like the flesh-eating zombies in the movies. These fiends will be able to run, think, and shoot, just like you and me."

Julianna swallowed hard. "A fate far worse than growing up without a mother could come to my son. I'm going to do everything I can to make sure that doesn't happen. Please don't stand in my way."

He wanted so badly to comfort her. "Okay. I'll talk to my mother. She can watch Cole while we're gone."

Julianna's rage toward Shane had long since dissipated. She almost smiled. "Thank you," she said, then walked away.

***

Early Tuesday morning, the first hint of dawn crested the mountains in the east. The air was still frigid even though spring was halfway over. Shane loaded the food, water, and ammunition into the back seat of his father's Ram 2500. Next, he placed a collection of empty plastic gas cans in the bed of the truck. Most were red. Some were yellow. They varied in size from one gallon to six. Shane pulled a blue tarp over the receptacles and placed several sticks of firewood to keep the tarp from blowing.

"That's the last of the fuel that can be siphoned out of your Sierra." Bobby approached the vehicle with a five-gallon gas can. "Are you sure you don't want to take my F-150? If it's just the two of us, we might get a little better mileage. We don't really need the mega-cab for a couple of backpacks."

Shane looked at Julianna's window but saw no evidence of light coming from inside. "I'm not entirely sure it's going to be just us."

"Oh!" Bobby's eyes grew wide as if he understood the situation. He poured the gas into the Ram's fuel tank. Afterward, he placed the empty container in the bed with the others. "You don't think a 5,000-gallon tanker is going to hold us for a while?"

"We don't have any diesel either. These few cans barely add up to 100 gallons, but it will make a difference."

"The refinery in Kentucky, you think they produce diesel?"

"They'll have access to it. Whether they trade for it, produce it, or procure it by some other means, they need diesel for delivery."

"What if they don't deliver? Maybe they just let the customers come to them."

"Then their customers will need diesel unless they're just filling up tanks one at a time. I can't imagine a refinery acting like a local filling station. They'd be missing out on too much business if they didn't offer diesel." Shane paused and looked toward the gate when he heard the noise of a vehicle on the gravel. "Someone is coming."

"It must be our people if Dan let them through the gate," Bobby replied.

"I hope you're right." Shane stared down the road and put his hand on his pistol. "It's a sheriff's department patrol vehicle."

Bobby stood beside Shane and looked on. "That thing is riddled with bullet holes. It's one of the cars that was on the front line at the elections."

"Then it has to be a friendly. Hammer and his men pulled their retreat with the vehicles farthest from the action. I doubt many of them had that much damage." Shane relaxed and walked out to meet the visitor.

Bobby walked beside him. "The car looks rough, but it lets potential attackers know that it won't be our first rodeo if they decide to engage with us."

The driver rolled down the window. Butterbean leaned his pudgy arm out the window. "Good morning Shane, Bobby."

"Butterbean, how are you?" Shane waved.

"I'm good. Eric and Johnny Teague are down the

road. They didn't want to try turning that big old tanker around on your property. Also, it's a two-seater. Would it be alright if I leave the patrol car in your driveway and ride with you?"

"Sure." Shane smiled. "We're happy to have you along."

"Thanks." Butterbean rolled up the window and parked the patrol car.

"I guess we'll need the mega-cab after all," Bobby joked.

Shane eyed his enormous friend. "I've never seen you riding in the back seat of a Smart car."

"Smart cars don't have back seats," Bobby retorted.

"I've never seen you in the front seat of one either," kidded Shane.

"I'm a different kind of big."

"Yeah, you're Twinkies-and-hot-dog big while Butterbean is more of a marshmallow-pie big."

"Don't knock Twinkies. They'll last longer than most of that long-term storage food you have in the basement." Bobby opened the passenger's door and placed his rifle inside. "Besides, we're not all genetically inclined to be built like a country music star."

"Twinkies last so long because they're synthetic." Shane loaded his weapon into the cab. "Nothing except humans will eat them. All the little micro-organisms and bugs that normally break down food into compost won't touch a Twinkie with a ten-foot pole."

"Why do you have to ruin Twinkies for me? Isn't this world hard enough?" Bobby got into the truck and closed his door.

Butterbean got in behind Bobby. "I don't know what you guys were talking about, but if it's something that's going to make me not like Twinkies, I don't want to know." He pulled his door shut. "Ignorance is bliss, my Grandmama would always say."

Shane had no desire to enter into the ring of debate with that particular belief. So, he said nothing and got into the cab. He heard the door behind him open and looked up at the rearview mirror.

Julianna yanked her door closed and smiled at Shane through the rearview mirror. "You weren't going to leave without me, were you?"

Shane feigned a smile and turned the key. "Of course, not. Glad to have you aboard."

Butterbean called over his hand-held radio. "Unit one, this is unit two. We're 10-17."

Eric Bivens voice came back over the radio. He seemed to be laughing. "10-4, unit two."

Shane looked up at the peculiar fellow diagonally behind him. "What's 10-17?"

"En route," said Butterbean.

"Could you not say en route? We're mostly civilians on this operation."

"I guess." Butterbean's voice seemed to deflate. "It's just that I memorized all them codes and never got to use 'em, being stuck inside at the jail all the time."

Shane felt like he'd just taken away Butterbean's favorite childhood toy. "On second thought, go ahead and use your special codes. Tell us what they mean, though. Maybe we can all learn them."

The pep returned to Butterbean's tone. "Thanks, Shane!"

They arrived at the bottom of the driveway. "Can I use the radio?" asked Shane.

"Sure," Butterbean handed him the portable unit.

Shane pressed the talk key. "We'll take the lead since we're a little more flexible if we have to make a quick turnaround. Stay back half a mile or so. That will give you time to react if we run up on some trouble."

"10-4," replied Johnny Teague.

Shane assumed the lead and glanced up to see the big red tanker follow. "Looks like you got a livestock gate stuck to your front bumper."

"I put it on there with baling wire," said the mayor's brother. "DIY grill guard."

"Deer are getting pretty thin. I doubt you'll need it. Although, it does make you look tough. Kinda gives your truck that Mad-Max look." Shane released the talk key.

Johnny Teague came back over the radio. "It ain't the deer I'm worried about."

The corners of Shane's mouth turned down as he recalled the myriad of horrors which could await them on the trip.

CHAPTER 19

Courage, then, my countrymen, our contest is not only whether we ourselves shall be free, but whether there shall be left to mankind an asylum on earth for civil and religious liberty.

Samuel Adams

Shane checked his mirrors regularly. His situational awareness was on high alert, scanning every turn and intersection for possible threats.

"You should have taken 441," said Julianna from the back seat. "I-40 is totally exposed."

"Normally, I'd agree with you. But 441 would take us within spitting distance of Knoxville." Shane watched Bobby turn to Julianna and speak in a hushed tone.

"Knoxville is where Shane was shot and Lilith was killed." Bobby glanced sympathetically at Shane as he turned to face the front.

"Oh, right," said Julianna. "Sorry, I forgot."

"It's okay," said Shane. "It's just that the interstate is less risky than getting so close to a large population center." He tried not to let the events of that harrowing day haunt his memory. He needed to stay focused.

All the passengers seemed aware of the danger involved in the excursion. Very little was said.

An hour into the trip and they'd encountered no problems. Shane broke the silence and pressed the talk key of the radio. "We'll get off just past Newport. We can take the backroads from there."

"Good choice," replied Johnny Teague.

Shortly thereafter, Shane called over the radio once more. "Guys, we just hit a long bridge. Someone has set up a roadblock at the end of it. Hold back and wait for me to call you back to tell you we're clear."

"I know the bridge," said Johnny. "That's Douglas Lake. If there's a roadblock, just turn around. We'll find another route."

"It's too late. The bridge arches. I didn't see the roadblock until we were halfway across. If they're hostiles, they'll have no problem running me down if I try to back out or turn around. I'm going to continue on across and hope it's just some good folks trying to keep their area safe."

"You've got two minutes to call me back and tell me it's all clear," Johnny replied. "Otherwise, we're coming in hot."

"How hot?" Shane slowed down as he approached the two vehicles blocking the road.

"We've got the full-auto rifles from the department," replied Johnny. "So, whatever you want to call it—extra spicy, I guess."

Shane placed the radio in the console and addressed the others in the cab with him. "Smile wide, be polite, and keep your fingers on the triggers."

He rolled down the window. "Good morning."

"Good morning to you," said one of the men who came out from behind the roadblock, which consisted of two pickups parked bumper to bumper. He held a pump-action shotgun. "Where ya'll headed?"

"Just passing through." Shane counted six more men holding various long guns behind the vehicles.

"Passin' through to where?" The man smiled, but his face showed that he was adamant about wanting more information.

"Going to see friends up near Huntington."

"Where you coming from?" The man looked in at the other passengers.

"Down near Whittier."

"Y'all look like you're going bear huntin'. Pretty well-armed, I mean."

"I've heard they've got bears up this way. Seems like you boys are keeping an eye out for predators as well."

The man smiled, revealing two teeth that were missing in the front of his mouth. "That's a long way, Whittier all the way to West Virginia. You must be sitting pretty with fuel."

"Not exactly. You might have heard, times are tough up in Huntington. We scraped together what gas we could find to get us up there. We're hoping to get our people and come on back."

"That's fine by me, but the toll to cross the bridge is five gallons. It covers our expenses in keeping the roads cleared and safe."

"Five gallons of gas?" Shane knew this was going south. "I'm sorry, we don't have it to spare. We'll back up and find another route."

"But you've already crossed the bridge. You still have to pay the toll."

Shane reached for his pistol.

The man raised his shotgun. "I wouldn't try that."

Shane looked to see all the other men leveling their weapons at his truck.

"Why don't you folks go ahead and step out of the vehicle?"

Shane couldn't let his team get out. They needed the safety of the vehicle for when Johnny and Eric showed up. "On second thought, why don't you fellows go ahead and help yourself to the fuel?"

"You've already shown your intentions of being a problem," said the man. "At this point, we need you to get out of the truck, nice and slow."

"If we do that, we're as good as dead." Shane kept his hand near his pistol. "If we're going to die, we'll be taking a few of you boys with us. Seeing how you're the one up front, I'm guessing you'll be one of the first to meet your maker.

"On the other hand, you could graciously accept

my apology, siphon out your five gallons, a little extra for your trouble, and we'll be on our way. We can all live to see another beautiful morning just like this one."

"Kenneth, come on up here with the gas can and the siphon hose." The man seemed to appreciate the compromise. "Bring 2 five-gallon cans. Fill 'em both up." He walked to the bed of the truck. He moved a few sticks of the firewood and pulled back a corner of the tarp. "Never mind on the gas cans, Kenneth. We'll use theirs. Just bring your siphon hose."

The man placed two fuel cans by the gas cap and stepped away from the truck. He joined his men in guarding Shane's team while Kenneth exacted the toll from the gas tank.

Shane rolled up the window. "Everyone, be ready."

"We're going to need that gas to get where we're going," Julianna said.

"I know. Let's hope it doesn't get spilled in the squabble." Shane held his pistol in his lap.

The loud horn of the fire department tanker blew. Shane glanced up to see the lights of the vehicle cresting over the arch of the bridge. He heard the siren screaming.

Butterbean squealed with excitement, "They're comin' in code three!"

Shane rolled down all four windows at once. "Eric and Johnny are taking a big risk to cause such a commotion. Let's make it count!" Shane slumped down in his seat, raised his pistol and shot the leader of the roadblock. He fell to the ground.

Shane raised up enough to see Kenneth who was holding the siphon hose in his hand and staring at the lights and sounds careening over the bridge. Shane hesitated for a moment, not wanting to shoot a man in the back, but they were outnumbered and chivalry had to take a back seat to survival. He squeezed the trigger twice. The Glock barked out two shots and Kenneth toppled beside the fuel cans.

The other men were confused by the big red vehicle barreling toward them. Some shot at the fire truck, others ran, but all seemed oblivious to Shane and the other passengers of the pickup who seized the opportunity to pick them off.

Two of the men who'd taken cover behind the roadblock vehicles realized what was happening. They redirected their fire to the Ram 2500, piercing the windshield.

"Keep shooting! Don't give them a chance to get a bead on any of us!" Shane put the truck in reverse and punched the gas pedal. The tires spun and eventually gained traction, pulling the pickup into the cloud of black smoke created by the spinning tires. Shane let off the gas, not wanting the truck to get out of control while perilously close to the edge of the bridge. He looked forward just in time to see the red lights and screeching siren of the tanker plow into the roadblock. The two trucks which had been parked nose to nose spun like billiard balls. One zipped backward, hitting the guardrail of the bridge and flipping over the low safety barrier. The other rotated twice, knocking down two men who'd been using the vehicle for cover.

Shane wasted no time. He put the pickup in park,

holstered his pistol, grabbed his rifle, and sprung from the cab.

He hustled to the sight of the impact and scanned the bodies for survivors. One man looked at Shane, reached for his pistol. POP, POP! Shane put two rounds in his skull.

Shane turned to see another of the men raising a shotgun. It was too late. He already had his bead set on Shane's chest. The man gave an evil smile. POW!

CHAPTER 20

For thou hast delivered my soul from death, mine eyes from tears, and my feet from falling. I will walk before the Lord in the land of the living.

Psalm 116:8-9

Shane closed his eyes. He heard the sound of the gun but didn't feel the impact. *Am I dead?* Shane ran his hand across his chest, feeling for blood and the multiple entry wounds which would come from such a close-range blast.

"Stay focused!" said a sweet familiar voice.

Shane opened his eyes to see Julianna lowering her rifle, going from body to body and placing two more rounds in each of them.

Bobby was right behind her, likewise making sure the men from the roadblock would be collecting no further tolls. Butterbean arrived eventually, ready to fight if need be.

"Check on Johnny and Eric!" Shane pointed to the tanker which had rolled to a stop just ahead.

Butterbean hurried toward the truck. Bobby quickly overtook him in getting to the heavy vehicle. He opened the driver's side door. Eric stepped out. Johnny emerged from the other side.

Shane glanced up from checking the corpses. "Are you guys alright?"

Johnny Teague made his way over to Shane. "Yeah, we just thought it was safer in the truck the way Julianna was out here shootin' folk. Thought you might have made her mad."

Eric approached them. "Domestic scuffles are some of the most dangerous situations for the boys in the department." He gave a mischievous grin. "Sometimes it's best if we give them a little time to cool off."

Julianna showed no amusement for the line of humor. "We'd have to first be domestic for there to be a scuffle. So, since no chance exists of the former coming about, I'd say you can rest at ease that neither will the latter."

Johnny winced in mock pain as he looked at Shane. "Ouch."

Shane pressed his lips together and glared at the comedian to offer his gratitude for the ill-timed jest. After being sure the other thieves were dead, Shane walked to the front of the fire truck to inspect it.

"Looks like you're going to need a new cattle gate." The tube-metal apparatus dangled from the bumper of the vehicle.

Johnny walked around to the front. "Nothing a little baling wire can't fix."

Shane looked back to the gas cans. "All that ruckus and those fuel containers didn't get knocked over."

Butterbean was closer to the receptacles. He picked them up and gasoline trickled out near the base of each. "No, but it looks like they caught some stray buckshot."

Shane frowned at having his good fortune dashed away so readily. "Bring that siphon hose. Let's see if we can squeeze any juice out of this lemon." He motioned toward the rusty old Chevy, which remained on the bridge.

Eric found a two-gallon plastic gas can, which had been knocked down the pavement by the impact. "Here's another container."

Johnny found another five-gallon can. "I've got one also."

Butterbean handed the orange siphon pump to Shane who placed one end of the long plastic tubing in the tank and the other inside the container which Eric had opened for him. Immediately, the gurgling sound of air mixing with liquid accompanied each stroke of the pump.

"Sounds like they were running on fumes." Shane attempted to push the hose deeper into the tank but acquired less than a gallon before it went dry.

"You've got a thirty-gallon tank on that Ram,

right?" asked Johnny.

"That sounds about right." Shane looked at the Dodge.

"You should have plenty to get you there," Johnny added.

Eric rubbed his chin. "What about the trip home? We're not even sure this place is operational. Even if it is, criminals may be in control of it."

Johnny said, "The line between an opportunistic businessman and a criminal is a tad murky at present. If we can get fuel, it might be best if we avoid labels."

Julianna rolled her eyes sardonically. "What a shame. Criminals and big business used to be so neatly delineated. No matter, we'll have Washington up and running again in no time. Then, the criminals can go back to hiring K-Street lobbyists to change the laws so they won't be considered criminals any longer."

Eric eyed the others. "It's a big risk. You have fuel to get home as it is. If we get there and this doesn't work out, we'll be in a pinch."

"I say we press on. The town needs this fuel." Julianna crossed her arms.

"She's right," said Johnny.

"We have enough fuel to bring back the tanker, but it's a two-seater. Getting us all back isn't a matter of comfort." He looked at Bobby and Butterbean. "It's simply not possible. I'd rather turn around, refuel Shane's truck and start out early tomorrow morning."

Butterbean seemed to recognize that because of his girth, he'd certainly not be one of the people coming back if the refinery wasn't open for business. "I agree with the sheriff. Better safe than sorry."

"Then you should have stayed home, Butterbean." Julianna glared at him. "Nothing about this trip was supposed to be safe. We could hit the same snag tomorrow. We might not even get as far as we did today."

"Let's put it to a vote. I'm with Julianna. I say we should push on." Johnny put his hand in the air.

"We're not that far from home. It's not a tremendous waste of resources to head back, regroup and set out again in the morning," said Eric Bivens.

"I'm sticking with the sheriff." Butterbean put his pudgy arm in the air and stepped closer to Eric in a showing of solidarity.

Shane realized the deciding vote was coming in his direction. He looked at Bobby. "What do you think?"

Bobby adjusted his rifle. "Whatever you say. I'm behind you 100%"

Shane appreciated Bobby's loyalty, but at this point, the decision sat squarely on his shoulders. He pondered the options for a moment. "Julianna is right. The road ahead is likely fraught with danger. We've traveled almost 100 miles. Giving that up is tantamount to ceding ground gained in battle, especially in light of the conflict we've just endured.

"I think we all agree that Jackson County needs this gas. This morning's event reminds us of how unhinged the country is coming. We have to be able to keep the sheriff's department mobile, not to mention fire and EMS. All the emergency services might be short staffed, but anything is better than nothing; particularly when it comes to maintaining a show of force against the marauders who are sure to come."

"I can't argue with that part," said Bivens. "I suppose if we get in a pinch, Julianna can ride back with us, and we'll send another vehicle to pick up you, Bobby, and Butterbean."

"I could hang on to the ladder on the back of the tanker for the way home." Butterbean's voice got higher.

"You can't ride on the back of the truck for 300 miles, Butterbean," Bivens said.

The hefty deputy seemed unwilling to proceed without an assurance that he would be able to return home. Butterbean looked over the side of the bridge. "There's more fuel cans down in the lake. Some of them look like they might be partially filled. Maybe we should try to get them."

Julianna looked over the guardrail. "Okay, why don't you hop on down there and try to get them out?"

His forehead showed his distress over the recommendation. "I'm not a very strong swimmer."

Shane also looked over the barrier. "Maybe he's right. If those were all empty, they'd be floating on top of the water. I see a few that are at least eighty percent under."

"That's going to take time," said Johnny. "We're already running behind schedule."

Shane looked back the way they'd come. He

spotted a boat ramp below the bridge. "This trip might take longer than we expected anyway. I don't want to give up resources unless we absolutely have to. You all wait here. I'll drive down there and try to fish them out."

"I'm a pretty good swimmer," Eric volunteered. "I'll come with you."

Shane started toward the truck. "Let's get going. This lake eventually empties out into the French Broad. The current is already pulling the fuel cans away from us."

Shane and the sheriff got in the pickup and drove to the lowest point of the boat ramp. Shane removed his boots and peeled off his clothes down to his boxer shorts. He looked up to make sure the rest of the team was watching out for them in case of attack. He saw Julianna looking over the guardrail. She quickly turned away.

Eric stripped down as well. "Early May, this mountain lake water is going to be chilly."

"Thanks for reminding me," Shane stepped into the frigid water. The coldness shot up to his back and into his bones. He forced himself forward and plunged in once he was deep enough. "It's not so bad once you're in."

"It's a crime to lie to a law enforcement officer," joked Bivens as he worked his way into the icy bath.

Shane chased after the nearest gas can as it floated farther and farther away. After a half an hour, Shane and Eric had managed to retrieve only two of the cans. The others were too far gone.

Shane hurried to put his clothes back on. "How

did you do?"

"Butterbean was right. This can is nearly full."

"Mine, too." Shane buttoned up his shirt. "Not only do we need the gas, but we also need the containers as well."

Once back up on the bridge, Shane and Eric helped the others collect the firearms from the fallen bandits. He held up the edge of the tarp for Julianna to place a load of guns beneath. "That was some good shooting earlier."

She eyed his shirt clinging to his wet torso then glanced back up at his eyes. She suppressed her smile. "You didn't do so bad yourself."

***

Shane glanced up at the rearview and addressed Julianna. "You should call my mom. Let her know that we're already running behind."

"Okay," she said. "When should I tell her to expect us?"

Bobby interjected. "By the time we get there and fill up the tanker, it will be getting close to dark. We might want to think about staying put and heading out first thing in the morning. If we're hitting this much trouble in the daytime, just think of how bad it could get at night."

Shane frowned. "I see your point, but I didn't pack any camping gear."

Bobby added, "Someone could sleep in the front seat and someone else in the back. Plus, another person could sleep in the cab of the tanker."

"I call dibs on the backseat!" Julianna leaned

forward.

"I guess that will be enough." Shane wanted to get this trip over with quickly, but not at the expense of unnecessary risk. "Three of us will need to stay awake to guard the trucks. Sleeping on the side of the road is only marginally safer than driving at night. We'll take four-hour shifts."

"Speaking of shifts, do you need me to drive for a while?" offered Bobby.

"Thanks, but I'm fine for now." Shane looked into the rearview again to see Julianna dialing the numbers on her phone.

"Should I say we'll be home tomorrow afternoon, then?" she asked.

"Yeah, that sounds good." Shane hoped they'd have no more surprises.

"Cell service is out—again," Julianna said.

"Try to send her a text," Shane replied.

Seconds later, Julianna said, "Nothing. I have no bars. I'm not even getting the unavailable message."

"We'll try again after a while," said Shane.

CHAPTER 21

But we also glory in tribulations, knowing that tribulation produces perseverance; and perseverance, character; and character, hope.

Romans 5:3b-4 NKJV

"This must be it." Shane pointed forward to the row of behemoth fuel tanks soaring six stories up, behind the three-story administration building. A labyrinth of pipes, steel structure frames, and liquid storage silos came into view on their right. The monstrous superstructure stood as a monument to the modern age which depended on the plant's refined petroleum products like a fish needs water.

"I think the military got here before we did. Look at the main gate." Butterbean indicated toward a tank sitting beside a row of MRAPs which formed a blockade to the entrance.

"I'm not so sure about that," Julianna said. "Those guards aren't wearing the same style camouflage. Their weapons don't even match. I don't think this is the military."

Shane called over the radio. "We're here, but we're trying to figure out if they are open for business. Why don't you guys hang back for a second? I'll call you when we know more."

"10-4," said Sheriff Bivens.

"Are we just going to drive up and ask them if they've got fuel for sale?" Bobby inquired.

"I think I'll drive by and come back around," Shane replied.

As the truck passed the main gate, Julianna said, "The guards watched us pass by. They had binoculars and were pointing at us."

Shane set his teeth together. "I don't like this."

"Maybe we should just go home. We've got fuel to get back," said Butterbean.

Shane continued up the road a ways. "Are they following us?"

"I don't see anything." Julianna turned backward in her seat.

"A big semi tanker just pulled out of the gate," Bobby watched his side view mirror.

Shane slowed down to let the big rig catch up to him.

"They've got escorts. Two Humvees," Julianna added.

Shane turned onto a side street to let the convoy pass. "Try to see what markings are on the tanker."

"It's a Walmart trailer, the tractor looks like an

owner-operator." Butterbean struggled to turn around.

"I'll take that as a good sign. Sounds like they're doing business." Shane called Johnny and Sheriff Bivens back over the radio. He relayed what they'd seen and informed them of his intentions. "If you don't hear back from me in five minutes, we're in trouble."

"I guess we'll bail you out again," said Johnny. "But remember, this will be twice in one day. Don't make a habit out of it."

Shane felt too anxious to enjoy the humor. "They've got MRAPs, a tank, and over thirty men guarding the gate. If we get in trouble, this will look nothing like the episode at the bridge."

Shane pulled into the access street. He said a short prayer, "God, please, watch over us. Get us through this and bring us home safely to our friends and family."

"Amen," Julianna echoed the sentiment.

Two guards wearing heavy body armor walked out toward the truck with guns low. One of them held up his hand signaling for Shane to stop.

Shane rolled down the window and kept his hands on the steering wheel.

"You folks lost?" The guard's voice was aggressive.

"No, sir. We're looking for gas."

"We're closed. Turn your vehicle around."

"I just saw a tanker pull out of here," said Shane. "And I couldn't help noticing that you've got a lot of firepower guarding a plant that supposedly isn't in operation."

"Regardless, we're not a gas station." The man remained hostile. "Turn your vehicle around and leave while you still can. We saw you creep by here a few minutes ago. If we see you driving around out here again, we'll kill you."

"I didn't mean to make you nervous." Shane held his hands up to show his willingness to comply. "And we're not looking for a fill-up. We have a 5,000-gallon tanker truck nearby."

"How nearby?"

"Right up the road. They're just waitin' for us to call and tell them that you're open for business."

"Who told you we're selling fuel?"

"We knew there was a refinery up this way. We took a chance and drove up from North Carolina."

"Where in North Carolina?"

Shane didn't feel comfortable telling them about Sylva, but he felt even more uneasy about trying to feed the man false information. "Jackson County."

"Call your tanker, have them come up."

"That means you're going to sell us gas?"

"It means we're going to have a talk."

Shane didn't like that response, but he didn't know what else to do. He called the tanker and relayed the situation.

"Pull through." The guard waved his hand and two of the large MRAPs moved back to create an opening.

Shane encouraged his team. "If they didn't want to trade, they wouldn't have let us in."

"Unless they want to rob us," Julianna said.

The guard held his hand up. "Do you have weapons in the vehicle?"

"We wouldn't have made it here without them."

"Leave them in the truck and step outside." The guard put his hand back on his rifle.

Shane felt less comfortable about how the meeting was progressing, but he had no other choice. "Okay, let's do what they ask."

The guards frisked Shane and the rest of the team. The lead guard motioned for Shane to step aside. "One of my men will drive your vehicle to the admin building."

Eric and Johnny soon arrived in the tanker. The guard also insisted that they leave their guns in the cab and exit the vehicle. Shane wondered if any of them were going to get out of this place alive.

Next, the guard came around and placed zip ties on each of their hands.

"Wait a minute! You said we were going to talk. Is this how you treat your prospective customers?" Shane protested.

"Standard security protocol." The guard took Shane by the arm and led him toward the administration building.

"Shane, I don't like this!" Julianna voiced her concern while being escorted by another guard.

Once inside the building, the guards led each of the six members of Shane's team to different rooms.

"Shane!" Julianna called out in fear.

"It's going to be okay. We'll get through this." He yelled out as she was whisked away behind a heavy metal door. Shane didn't entirely believe his own statement, but he was powerless to do anything other than issue false promises.

Shane was gruffly put into a room alone and the

door was locked. He examined the room. It had formerly been an office with a view into the parking lot. He watched guards going through their belongings in the tanker and the pickup. The glass was not reinforced and had no bars on the outside. If his hands were not restrained, he could easily break the glass and make a run for it.

"They'd gun me down in ten seconds flat. Where would I go? Even if I could, I can't abandon Julianna and the others."

Shane waited for what seemed like hours. His mind raced. He pressed his arm against the wall, attempting to push his opposite wrist out far enough from behind his back to see his watch. He could not. The plastic restraint would not allow him a glimpse. He sighed with exasperation and took a seat in the simple chair.

Finally, he heard the sound of a key going into the lock. He stood back up to see who was entering the room. A guard dressed in camouflage and a man wearing all black came in.

"How long are you going to keep me chained up like an animal?" His brow set in heavy furrows.

The man in black placed a clipboard on the table. "That depends on you."

"Since when did Marathon Oil start taking people hostage?"

"Marathon isn't currently in charge of this facility."

"Then who is? You're obviously not military."

"No, sir. We're not." The man motioned to the chair Shane had been sitting in. He sat in the other chair while the guard stood by the door. "Why don't you sit down?"

Shane reluctantly complied. "Who are you people?"

"More importantly," asked the man, "who are you?"

"Shane Black."

The man looked at him curiously for a moment. "Wait a minute. Ain't you the fellow who played guitar for Backwoods?"

"Yeah, that's me. Now can you cut this tie off my wrists?"

"Not just yet. Lots of people who were fine, upstanding citizens prior to the meltdown have become hardened criminals. Why are you here?" The man continued questioning Shane for the next several minutes.

"Are you going to let me go?" Shane asked when the interview had finished.

"If everyone on your team gives the same story, you'll all be released."

"Then what?"

"Then you can meet with the administrator."

Shane hoped everyone's version of the truth would line up. "What if someone on my team gets jittery and tries to be evasive with the questioning?"

"Then it won't end well for any of you, Mr. Black." The man opened the door and the guard followed him out.

Shane heard the deadbolt click. The locks had been modified to require a key on each side. He was stuck until further notice.

CHAPTER 22

It's not the size of the dog in the fight, it's the size of the fight in the dog.

Mark Twain

Shane's mind had grown numb from anticipation. His arms ached from being in the same position for so long. He felt sure the sun should be setting by now, but it still hung high. Having no other means to pass the time, he stared out the window.

He heard the sound of a key going in the lock. Once again, he stood up. The man in black had returned with the same guard. Shane waited apprehensively to hear if he'd been exonerated, or if Butterbean had perhaps tried to throw the captors off the scent by telling them that they were from

Boone or another town. One misstep could cost them all their lives.

"Turn and face the wall, Mr. Black," said the man.

Shane's heart raced. This didn't sound promising. However, he was in no position to complain about the request. He did as he'd been asked.

He felt the guard grab his hands and lift them up. Then suddenly, the restraints fell away.

"Follow me," said the man.

Shane turned, rubbed his wrists, which were red from the plastic bands, and followed the man out the door. He led Shane up two flights of stairs, down a hall, and to a door. The guard rapped gently.

"Come on in," said a voice from inside.

The man opened the door. "Mr. Creech, this is Shane Black."

A robust fellow sat behind a large wooden desk. His prosthetic mechanical hand, made of two hooks, which could be manipulated for simple tasks, held a large smoldering cigar. He wore an average plaid shirt and a baseball hat, which had a blue-and-white USW emblem on the front. His beard was wiry and mostly gray. He took a puff of his cigar and stood up. "The legendary Shane Black. To what do I owe the honor?"

Shane inspected the name bar on the desk, which read *Caleb Creech*. "Mr. Creech, we had come in peace looking to purchase gasoline. But I'll have to be honest, your consumer relations department leaves something to be desired."

Creech started to laugh, but his chuckle gave

way to a coughing fit. Diminishing puffs of smoke followed each of his successive hacks. "Balancing security with a pleasurable customer experience has proven to be something of a sticky wicket.

"We've been attacked three times. The latest assault came after a band from Cincinnati came to scope us out. They posed as representatives of a small municipality just outside of the city." Creech looked out his giant corner-office glass window which provided a view of the entire facility and the mountains beyond. "I lost five of my best men in that shootout. Of course, they lost all of theirs."

Creech turned back to Shane. "I wish things were different, but I can't apologize for keeping my people safe. We'll always have customers. Our product is in high demand—as evidenced by your own treacherous journey. You didn't risk your lives on the open road for butter or sugar. If you're offended by our astringent measures, you and your people are free to leave."

Shane lowered his gaze. The man was correct. Caleb Creech was in charge of the one commodity which could maintain Sylva's status as a going concern. "I'd still like to do business with you, Mr. Creech."

"Provided you can produce an agreeable means of payment, I'm inclined to accept your business." The man returned to his seat and took another long puff from his cigar. "But real quickly, we do not issue credit."

"No sir, I don't expect that you do," Shane said.

"Then have a seat, Mr. Black." Creech motioned to the chair in front of the desk.

"The man who interviewed me said that you're not affiliated with the prior operators of the plant. Do you mind if I ask who your organization is?" Shane sat down.

Creech smiled. "No, I suppose not. When the dollar collapsed, the company had no means to meet payroll. The workers realized the country would still need gasoline to keep it running, so they continued to come in. Once it became apparent that the gold dollar wasn't going to hold up, the workers requested that the plant pay them in fuel. It seemed like an amicable solution to us. Management refused the offer. We could have simply walked, but by that time, paychecks were several weeks in arrears. The company owed us our wages. So, we handed management their pink slips."

"Doesn't that usually go the other way?" asked Shane.

"Usually," Creech laughed. "But times were changing and so were the standard ways of doing business."

Shane wondered if *pink slip* was a euphemism for *a bullet in the head* but didn't ask for clarification on the matter. "NPR said something about the government nationalizing the refineries on the Gulf Coast. They never tried to step in here?"

"Oh, they tried. But what they were offering to the workers amounted to little more than slave labor. So, we all went home. Let 'em have it."

"What happened? Why did they pull out?" Shane inquired.

"Because they're the federal government, son. Those people can't tie their own shoelaces without a forty-five-page manual. If they had the sense required to run an oil refinery, we wouldn't be in this pickle in the first place. Use your head, boy."

Shane saw the financial collapse as more of a lack of political will to do the right thing than an issue of intelligence, but he supposed the man's opinion was at least partially merited. "So when they left, you and the other workers came back in?"

"Yep."

Shane pointed to the man's hat. "Were you with the union?"

"Yes, sir. I worked at this plant for ten years before I had my accident." Creech opened and closed his mechanical claw. "Been head of the local union for the past twenty. I couldn't perform my regular duties without all ten digits."

"I understand," said Shane. "What forms of payment are you accepting?"

"Oh, you know, the usual. Guns, ammo, food. My men went through your vehicles."

"Yeah, I watched through the window," frowned Shane.

"Part of that was to see what your intentions were on coming here. The other part was to see what you had to trade. I can give you a premium price for those two fully-automatic rifles that were in the tanker, but we're a long way from 5,000 gallons. Even if we take all the weapons you brought, you'd only be around 2,000 gallons."

"We weren't planning to trade for the guns," said Shane.

"I don't see anything else of value. You weren't thinking of sticking us up, were you?" Creech's brows sank lower on his forehead.

"Absolutely not." Shane began to unzip his boot.

The guard quickly raised his rifle.

Shane put his hand up. "It's okay, I'm getting a coin out from under my insole."

Creech waved at the guard. "Put 'em down, Mickey."

Shane pulled the insole out of his boot and retrieved the one-ounce gold coin. "Do you take real money?"

Caleb Creech sat up and inspected the item. "What the devil is that, a monkey?"

Shane hoped his choice of animals wouldn't sour the deal. "It's minted by the Bank of Singapore. I converted some of my cash into gold at the last minute. All the really nice-looking coins were gone with the exception of some European coins."

Creech pulled a magnifying glass out of his desk and examined the coin further. "Why didn't you bring me one of them?"

Shane pressed his mouth in a straight line. "They're fractional, roughly a fifth ounce of gold in each, and have a higher percentage of alloy metals like silver. This coin is 24 carat."

"It's gold, alright. I'm familiar with pre-33 gold. I don't mind that they're 10 percent alloy. They wear better for circulation."

Shane saw the fact that Creech was familiar with gold coins as a positive sign. "So, you'll accept gold for payment?"

Caleb Creech looked up from the magnifying glass, which he held with his mechanical hand. "The Arabs are taking it, so I reckon I am, too."

Shane presented his case for the valuation of 5,000 gallons of gasoline in gold.

Creech smiled. "You've done your homework. Most folks who've seen you prancing around at the Grammys would never expect you to be such a good horse trader."

Shane wasn't sure if he should take the comment as an insult or a compliment. "So, five ounces for 5,000 gallons. Can you make that happen for me?"

"Anyone who's ever been at the bargaining table knows you don't open with your best offer."

Shane grinned. "I've always had an agent, so don't overestimate my negotiation skills."

"All that aside, this isn't the international market. We're operating in an increasingly hostile environment and add to our risk every time we start selling to another group."

"How so?"

"You could tell every Larry, Moe, and Curly along the way where you obtained your resources."

"I wouldn't do that. It wouldn't be in my best interest to increase demand."

"If you had a gun to your head, you might."

"If I have a gun to my head, I already know where to send them." Shane knew better than to start bargaining with a veteran union boss. "So, what's the price? In gold?"

"If you've got five ounces, I'll give you 1,500 gallons."

"No way. I'll make a run down to the Gulf."

"Be my guest. If you think my offer is unfair, try striking a deal with the feds. They might just decide to nationalize your five ounces. It won't be the first time they've confiscated gold. That's if you even make it down there without being killed."

Shane stood up and walked toward the door. "I'll take my chances. Government has a history of waste, fraud, and abuse when it comes to handling resources. I'm pretty sure I can find an administrator over one of the refineries looking for a bonus. Thank you for your time, Mr. Creech. Can you direct me to where the rest of my group is being held?"

Caleb Creech showed no remorse over the loss of business. "Sure. Mickey, will you take Mr. Black to his friends and see that they find their way out?"

"Yes, sir." The guard opened the door and escorted Shane down the hall. They descended the stairs, returning to the first floor. Shane was taken to a room that looked like it might have been a cafeteria at one time. Julianna, Butterbean, and the others were sitting at a table together sipping coffee from Styrofoam cups.

Julianna jumped up from the table. "Shane!" She rushed to his side and hugged him. "They didn't tell us where you were or what you were doing. I thought something might have happened to you."

Shane embraced her, but she quickly pulled away. "I was talking to the administrator." He looked at his team. "No one was hurt or injured while we were separated?"

"Just my pride," joked Johnny Teague.

Shane tried to smile in the face of total failure. "Let's get going."

"What happened?" quizzed Eric Bivens. "Are they going to sell us any gas?"

"No," Shane replied. "He's asking too much."

"Why? How much is he charging?" Bivens inquired.

"He offered 1,500 gallons for five ounces."

"So we could have gotten 3,000 gallons. That's more than half the tanker." Sheriff Bivens walked next to Shane as they were taken back to their vehicles.

"Yeah." Shane began to regret his hardline approach.

Eric Bivens continued to try persuading him. "It's your gold, Shane, but that could have gone a long way in fueling our patrol cars. Plus, the rolling blackouts are getting worse. If we completely lose power, we'll need generators to run water pumps and other critical machinery."

Shane said nothing. He got into his vehicle and closed the door.

Julianna powered on the phone which had been taken from her at the beginning of the interrogations. "I hate to add insult to injury, but phone service is still out. We've never had an outage last all day."

"That's just great." Shane led the way to the exit. As he waited for the two MRAPs to pull away from each other, he wished he could go back to the negotiating table.

One of the guards spoke over a walkie-talkie. He held his hand up for Shane to wait a little longer. He looked at the pickup, then walked toward the driver's side door.

Shane rolled down his window. "Is there a problem?"

"Mr. Creech wants to have another word with you before you leave."

Shane wasn't sure if that were a good thing or a bad thing. But with two large armored vehicles blocking his exit, it really didn't matter. He was going to give Creech the time he'd requested. "Okay."

CHAPTER 23

The curious task of economics is to demonstrate to men how little they really know about what they imagine they can design.

Friedrich Hayek

Shane walked back into the large corner office. "Mr. Creech, you wanted to see me?"

"I wish I'd had someone like you at the table for all those contract negotiations. You've got guts, son. Or, you're just plain stupid. We both know you'd never survive a trip down to the Gulf and back. At least not without a lot more firepower and personnel than you brought on this trip. Let's cut to the chase. What's the best you can do if I fill up your truck?"

A renewed sense of life raced through Shane's veins. His eyes lit up. He hoped he'd not lost his edge. He felt eager to seize his second chance but remembered not to open with his highest bid. "I'd have to talk to my colleagues, but we'd probably be willing to go as high as seven ounces."

Creech shook his head as if disappointed in Shane. "Come on, boy! What's all this business about your colleagues? Either you have the authority to act or you don't. If I'm talking to the wrong person, get out of my office and put me in touch with the decision maker. Maybe I had you all wrong. I can't believe you made a rookie mistake like that. You have to be assertive and be in charge. You're not talking to an electronics salesman at the local big box store. This ain't about getting ten bucks knocked off a television."

Shane hated being belittled by the man who'd spent the past two decades in heated contract negotiations. But he figured the advice was solid, should he find himself in a similar situation. "I'll go eight. That's as high as I can go."

Creech smiled. "That's better. I'll fill you up for fifteen."

"Fifteen? That was your original offer!"

"No, it's not. Originally, I offered you 1,500 gallons for five ounces. Fifteen would have only bought you 4,500 gallons. I'm throwing in another 500 gallons."

"How generous. But we don't have fifteen ounces. I'll give you nine ounces, but I'll need the fuel tanks of the tanker topped off with diesel. Plus,

I have about 100 gallons in fuel containers that I'll also need to be filled with diesel."

"What makes you think we have diesel? This is a gasoline refinery."

"You must have access to it. You'd be a fool not to. I can't imagine a man who's managed to pull off all of this would let such an opportunity pass him by."

Creech neither confirmed nor denied the assumption. "Twelve ounces."

"I don't have twelve ounces."

"How much do you have? Because I'm getting pretty close to telling you to quit wasting my time."

Shane reiterated his needs. "If you can top off the tanker's fuel tanks, the cans, and the 5,000 gallons, I have 11 ounces of gold. The monkey, plus ten more."

Caleb Creech turned his back to Shane. He surveyed the operations under his command as if pondering the deal. "Bring me the gold."

"Do we have a deal?"

"I'm not accepting such a ridiculously low price without seeing the physical metal. I'll make up my mind when I see the coins."

Shane hoped this was going to work. "Then I'll be right back."

"I think I'll join you if you don't mind." Creech walked down to the vehicles with Shane.

"Not at all." Once back to the parking lot, Shane took out the tire tool and lowered the spare tire from beneath the bed of the Ram.

"Clever place to put it," Creech said.

"Thanks." Shane began letting out the air.

"Bobby, can you bring me the pry bar under the seat?"

"Sure thing." Bobby handed him the instrument.

Shane pushed the tire off the rim and extracted a small plastic tube. He handed it to Creech.

Caleb Creech opened the container. His eyes sparkled as he looked at the various coins.

"Do we have a deal?"

The old union boss held out his good hand. "Where's the monkey?"

Shane pulled it from his pocket and placed it in Creech's palm.

The refinery administrator nodded to one of the guards. "Have the boys fill up the tanker. Then top off the fuel tanks with diesel. He's got some fuel cans in the back of his pickup. Load those up with diesel also."

Shane tried to contain his elation. He held out his hand. "Thank you, sir. It's going to mean a lot to our county."

Creech shook his hand and gave Shane a genuine smile. "I had fun bargaining with you. You're pretty good—for a rookie. I didn't mean to rattle you. It's just in my nature to fight like a pit bull when I'm at the negotiation table."

Shane watched Creech's men drive off with his vehicles. The thought crossed his mind that they might not come back with them. But if Creech intended on pulling a fast one, he'd had many other opportunities to do so. "Could I ask you for one small favor?"

Caleb Creech tucked the tube of gold coins in his pocket. "Small being the operative word." His facial stance returned to that of the rugged negotiator. "Let's hear it."

Shane looked at the sun dipping low over the hills in the west. "We had planned to be in and out. When we set out this morning, we hoped to be home shortly after sunset. The roads will only get more dangerous after dark. Would you consider allowing us to sleep in the parking lot tonight? We'll be out of your hair at first light."

Creech rubbed his gray beard with the metallic hooks of his prosthetic hand.

Shane attempted to spin the request. "It's in your own best interest. We'd like to establish a long-term-trading relationship. We'll be producing crops as the summer moves on. Our county is predominantly agricultural land, so we can produce much more than we can consume. Being across the river from Huntington, West Virginia, I'm sure you could find a market for such commodities."

Creech nodded slowly. "Lots of hungry folks over there already. And I suppose I'm partly to blame for y'all getting' out so late. I'll do you one better. Y'all can sleep in the offices. We've got a few army sleeping bags in a storage container near the back of the property. I'll have the boys bring some up for you. We have running water in the bathrooms. No showers, but you can take a cat bath in the sink."

"We'd really appreciate that," said Shane.

Creech added, "They're bringing in a hog they've had smokin' all day. BBQ baked beans as well. Why don't y'all come on in the cafeteria and join me for dinner?"

"I appreciate your hospitality, but we brought MREs," said Shane.

"Nonsense! I won't hear of it. Y'all come on in here and get you something to eat."

Shane and the others followed the rough-cut gentleman into the cafeteria area. They helped themselves to water and sweet tea, then sat at a large round table with Creech.

While they waited for the food to be brought out, Julianna asked, "Doesn't the local law enforcement give you trouble about having such a large militia? You've got tanks, MRAPs, and we counted at least forty security personnel. That's just for one shift."

Creech laughed. "Darlin', there wouldn't be no law enforcement if it weren't for me. Not in Catlettsburg nor Huntington, neither one. Might not even be towns left by now. Oh, they've both got sheriffs, and mayors, and all. But them boys answer to me." Creech tapped his chest with the cold steel fingers of his mechanical hand.

The slow-roasted pig was brought into the dining facility. Shane and the others enjoyed a sumptuous southern feast with Caleb Creech, then washed up and headed to their rooms.

Shane looked in on Julianna. "Are you going to be okay in here by yourself?"

She sat in the corner of the room on the unrolled olive-green sleeping bag. She looked at him but didn't answer.

Shane knew he was about to step in a mess, but his heart wouldn't let his mouth stay shut. "I could sleep in here, if you want me to. I'll stay on the other side of the room. If it will make you feel safer."

She looked at him a while longer. Finally, she gave a faint nod.

Shane's heart raced at the thought of sleeping in the same room with her. He'd never expected her to agree to the proposition. "I'll get my things and be right back."

***

Early Tuesday morning, the team loaded up their weapons and belongings into the vehicles and rolled out. Rested, fed, and with the mutual feeling of great accomplishment, they headed back on the road. Shane hoped the trip home wouldn't be as treacherous as the journey to the refinery.

Shane put his sunglasses on as the morning sun crested over the mountains in the east. He pressed the talk key. "Johnny, I appreciate your bravery and determination, but if we hit another roadblock, we might have to rethink slamming into it head-on with 5,000 gallons of fuel."

Johnny chuckled. "10-4, good buddy."

"Are we taking the same route home?" asked Butterbean.

"I was planning on it. We didn't have any more trouble after the bridge. Those guys won't be bothering us again."

Bobby laughed. "Those guys won't be bothering anybody again."

"It just makes me nervous, going back over Douglas Lake," Butterbean commented.

"Any route we take is going to make me

nervous. But better the devil you know than the one you don't."

"I'd rather not see any devils," said the plump deputy.

"Me, too," Shane laughed. He glanced in the rearview. "Has anyone been able to get a cell signal?"

Julianna checked her phone. "Still nothing."

"Mom and the others are probably worried sick about us." Shane said a silent prayer asking God to get them home with no further incidents.

Bobby clicked on the radio. "Let's see if NPR has anything to say about cell phone outages."

"The only good thing that might have come out of the collapse is that NPR has been forced to focus on hard news rather than promoting the extreme leftist agenda," said Shane.

"They still manage to sneak it in," replied Julianna. "Just listen to the way the reporters ascribe blame to capitalism and suggest that a more socialist government would have managed the crisis better."

Shane added, "The world would never know, except that we have so many great historical case studies like Russia, Zimbabwe, Venezuela, even Argentina had some very socialist economic policies. The only blame you can validly tack on capitalism is the crony capitalism which has enriched its patrons through monetary creation to promote special interests. Once again, made possible by the left through a burgeoning federal government. A smaller government would never have had the power to debase the currency to the point of collapse.

After a half an hour of Jazz Blues, a news report finally aired. The soft-spoken male reporter said, "A UN special counsel has put together a new triumvirate committee to address the failed US economy. With global currencies teetering on the verge of a catastrophic downfall, the UN has assumed a more forceful stance toward America. The old triumvirate tasked with monitoring the gold dollar was unsuccessful in reviving the failed reserve currency, so the US Federal Reserve will not have a role in the new committee. This new organization will possess greater power to act on behalf of the global economy and will be made up of three custodians, individuals chosen from the IMF, World Bank, and UN. IMF Managing Director Maris Allard will act as the committee's chairperson and will have the most authority of any of the three technocrats assigned to what is being termed as the Economic Sustainability Commission. Ms. Allard will work hand in hand with President Donovan in solving America's most challenging issues. The Donovan Administration has already agreed to the partnership with full support from House and Senate leaders. All additional aid to the US hinged on acceptance of the deal so the White House and Congress had few alternatives.

"No specific measures have been released officially, but Ms. Allard had been recommending that the US consider scrapping all wealth-transfer programs as well as selling off all military equipment except for the most rudimentary weapons and vehicles necessary for national defense.

"Pundits believe that under the new deal, the IMF will step in as the de facto administrator over US-based defense companies who sell to other nationalities. Previously arranged commission rates between those companies and the Pentagon will still apply, but the IMF will have sole discretion in managing those funds.

"Maris Allard has also gone on record suggesting that the US intelligence apparatus offer its services for a fee to UN member nations with Most-Favored-Nation status. Likewise, she has said the US should offer for sale federally owned lands, which make up some 650 million acres, most of which are in the western states.

"The details of this morning's agreement have not been released to the public yet, but it is thought that these terms are likely included in the pact between the US and the Economic Sustainability Commission.

"This has been an NPR news brief. We will report more on the ESC's new measures and forthcoming aid packages as the details become available."

Shane cut off the radio. "That's what bankruptcy looks like."

Julianna said, "Bankruptcy? That only applies to the people you owe money to. Wasn't most federal debt held by US institutions and individuals? China owned about 10% at one point, but they got smart and stopped rolling over their bonds when they matured."

"In the classical sense of the word, yes, you're right. But think of an individual who's been living on credit cards for ten years. Even though he's been flat broke for the entire decade, he's able to borrow from Peter to pay Paul. Until suddenly, Peter stops lending him money. Now what is he going to do? His McMansion still needs electricity. His Maserati still needs gas. He still has to eat. Being completely penniless, he has to start hocking assets to meet immediate needs. He can stick Peter with the credit card bill and maybe never have to give him a red cent. But from this point forward, no reputable lender will loan him a dime. Once our buy-now-pay-later borrower hits rock bottom, his dependency on liquidity doesn't go away. It's still there, but now, he has to go to the darkest alleys for cash. He starts with pawnshops and title loan companies until he has nothing left of value. His last stop is the loan shark where non-payment means a black eye, a broken leg, or something a little more permanent.

"Pol Pot and Chavez were both socialist. We can agree that both brought about undesirable outcomes, but your chances of surviving were somewhat more advantageous under Chavez. Just as there are different levels of socialism, bankruptcy can vary greatly from case to case."

"So, are you trying to tell us we're getting more of a Khmer-Rouge version of bankruptcy?" asked Bobby.

Shane frowned. "We're still riding the slippery slope all the way to the bottom. We can't really assess how bad it's going to get until we hear the final thud."

"Well, that makes me feel better," laughed Bobby.

"Where did you learn all of that?" Butterbean asked.

"His father," Julianna said. "He used to drill that stuff into him."

Shane remembered fondly the Sunday dinners of years ago when Julianna would come over after church. She seemed to enjoy listening to his dad talk about politics and economics. And Paul Black certainly enjoyed talking about the subjects.

***

The team hit no obstacles on the way home. No ambushes, no roadblocks, and none of the threats which Shane had worried so much about. Johnny Teague and Eric Bivens turned off from following Shane at the Teague family compound less than a mile from the Blacks' farm.

Shane breathed a sigh of relief as he pulled up the long gravel driveway. He looked up the hill where the grand chinked-log cabin had stood amongst the trees like a fairytale image and his heart stopped.

"What happened?" Julianna screeched. "Cole!"

Shane raced the truck up the hill to the smoldering pile of ash, scorched timber beams, and rubble, where his family home had been for so long.

CHAPTER 24

And, behold, there came a great wind from the wilderness, and smote the four corners of the house, and it fell upon the young men, and they are dead; and I only am escaped alone to tell thee. Then Job arose, and rent his mantle, and shaved his head, and fell down upon the ground, and worshipped, And said, Naked came I out of my mother's womb, and naked shall I return thither: the Lord gave, and the Lord hath taken away; blessed be the name of the Lord. In all this Job sinned not, nor charged God foolishly.

Job 1:19-22

Shane ran toward the ashes. In his distress, he reached for one of the charred beams. Bobby grabbed him from behind in a bear hug. He lifted him from the ground and pulled him backward. Butterbean had to likewise restrain Julianna who was screaming for her child hysterically.

"I have to get in there!" Shane yelled.

"Shhh, take it easy. Calm down," said Bobby. "That pile of rubble is unstable. And it's hot enough to cook you in about ten seconds flat."

"Cole... my mom... I have to get in there."

"Relax, relax," Bobby coaxed. "You don't know that they were in there. You'll only make things harder on them if you try to go in."

Shane's mind soon came to grips with the fact that if anyone were in that fire, he could do nothing to help them. He ceased struggling against Bobby. A tear came to his eyes. His sorrow was accentuated by Julianna's woeful wails. He turned to see her burying her face in Butterbean's shoulder.

"It's okay, Julianna, it's alright. Everything is going to be fine." Butterbean patted her on the shoulder.

Shane looked around for signs of survivors. He saw none. "Let's go to the little house and the trailers. Someone must know something." He knew it would be the best thing for Julianna as well. "Come on, let's go look. Cole could be at the guest cabin with Angela and my mother."

"Why wouldn't they have come out here by now? They'd have heard us pull in!" She seemed genuinely confused.

"I don't know. Let's just get in the pickup and

drive down there. We'll get this all figured out." Shane led her to the truck and helped her in the passenger's seat. Bobby rode in the back with Butterbean. Shane drove first to the guest cabin. Still sobbing, Julianna got out and accompanied him to the door. Shane knocked, but no one answered. He used his key to let himself inside.

The others followed him into the cabin. "Wasn't your sister staying in this room?" asked Bobby. "It looks like it's been cleaned out."

Shane looked in the empty closet. "Let's go check the trailers."

Julianna raced out the door ahead of everyone else. Leaving the pickup at the guest cabin, Shane sprinted to keep up with her. She frantically went from door to door, banging on the entrance of each of the mobile residences. "It's no use. No one is here."

Shane grabbed her and pulled her to himself. She cried on his shoulder. He stroked her head tenderly. "We can't assume the worse. We know that everyone wasn't burnt up in the fire. The others have gone somewhere. Cole is probably with them."

She looked up at him, as if she wanted to believe. "That's just an assumption."

Bobby and Butterbean drove the pickup to the clearing where the trailers were stationed. The two of them exited the vehicle. "Nothing?" Bobby asked somberly.

Shane shook his head in despair. He heard the sound of tires on the gravel road. "Quick! Get the rifles!" All of them scurried to the cab of the vehicle to retrieve their weapons.

Butterbean held up his hand and lowered his weapon. "It's the sheriff."

Shane stepped out from cover and waved. The vehicle had passed his location but expeditiously backed up. Shane walked down to the road to meet the vehicle. The others followed him.

Eric Bivens and the Teague brothers exited the SUV.

"Mayor, did you hear anything last night?" Shane asked.

Jimmy Teague nodded with a solemn face. "I'm afraid so."

"What happened?" Julianna implored.

"There was a fire in the middle of the night."

Shane asked, "Did everyone get out?"

Jimmy lowered his gaze. "I'm afraid not."

Shane's stomach sank. He put his arm around Julianna and pulled her close. "Cole? Is Cole alive?"

"Yes," said Jimmy. "He and your sister went with the pastor and Dan's family. Dan said you'd know where they went. Toward Murphy."

Shane said, "Yeah, I know where they went."

"Mrs. Perkins and Mrs. Farris didn't make it." The mayor lightly shook his head. His eyes seemed to be tearing up. "Neither did your mother."

Shane's heart stopped. He felt his face growing pale. He felt light-headed.

"Why don't you have a seat?" Bivens helped Shane sit down on the back seat of the vehicle, his legs still turned outward.

"What happened?" Shane asked in unbelief.

The mayor continued, "She brought Cole out,

then went back inside to wake up Maggie Farris and Mrs. Perkins."

Shane shook his head. "Why was Maggie Farris in the house?"

"Angela said something about her missing Fulton, feeling lonely, that sort of thing. I suppose your mother had invited her to stay the night so she wouldn't be alone in the trailer."

"Why did the rest of them leave?" Shane struggled to process the chain of events.

The mayor frowned. "An envelope was nailed to the tree at the entrance of your driveway. It was from Hammer. He said if Eric and I don't step down, things are only going to get worse."

Shane stood up, pressed his teeth together, and clinched his fists. Tears began to stream down his face. "So it was Hammer. Arson. He killed my father, and now he's murdered my mom."

"I'm so sorry, Shane." Julianna stood by him. She embraced his hand.

Jimmy popped the rear hatch of the SUV. "We took up a collection for clothing around the Teague compound. There's a good many of us, and we come in all shapes and sizes. Hopefully some of this stuff will fit. These two bags are for Julianna and Cole. Here's one for you."

Shane kept his bag. The other two he handed off to Julianna. He felt something against his leg. Looking down, he saw Sorghum. "Mrs. Perkins' cat."

Bobby reached down and picked her up. "I guess you're down to eight lives."

"We can keep the cat over at our place if you

want," Johnny offered.

Shane dried his eyes. "No. We'll take her. Cole likes the cat. She'll be a comfort to him." He turned his eyes to the charred hilltop where ribbons of smoke trailed toward the late-afternoon sky. "Has anyone tried to pull out any remains?"

"It's too dangerous," said Jimmy. "You'll have to wait until at least tomorrow before you can go diggin' around in there."

"What are we going to do about Hammer?" asked Shane.

"Take the day to mourn. Go see the others and get a good night's rest," Eric put his hand on Shane's back. "We'll talk about all of that tomorrow."

"Why don't you let me drive out to Murphy?" said Bobby.

Shane nodded but said nothing.

"I'm awful sorry, Shane." Butterbean's face showed his sympathy. "Y'all take care. I'll see you later." He began the long walk up the hill to retrieve his patrol vehicle.

After the Teagues and Sheriff Bivens had offered their condolences, Shane let Julianna and Bobby lead him back to the pickup.

***

Tuesday night, Shane numbly poked at the campfire thinking of the carrion left in the wake of his mistakes. He sat on a rough bench made of a wide board setting upon two low sections of a log acting as the supports.

Cole sat next to him outside of the old illegal distillery which now served as his group's safe house. "Do you miss Grandma Black?"

Shane forced a smile. "I do."

His son put his head on his shoulder. "Me, too. But she's in Heaven with Grandpa Black now. She missed him. Aren't you happy that they can be together?"

"I'm trying to be, but it's going to take a little time. Right now, I wish they were both still here. But I'm glad you're safe."

"I wish I had known she was my grandma before." The young boy found another stick to poke at the fire with his father. "Grandpa Black, too."

The guilt of robbing the child of getting to know his grandparents weighed on Shane like a heavy chain. Added to his grief, it felt unbearable. He knew the boy had not meant to hurt him, but like the final proverbial straw on the camel's back, it simply crushed what little remained of his spirit. Shane turned away from Cole, hoping that he wouldn't see his tears.

Julianna returned from her shower. "Cole, it's time for bed."

"Okay, mama." The boy put his arms around Shane's neck.

He swallowed hard, pushing down the emotion. He embraced the lad. "Good night, Cole."

"Good night, Shane." He trotted off with Julianna toward their little spot in the barn.

Left alone with his thoughts, Shane was free to grieve. Free to regret. Free to wish in vain that he could turn back time. So many things he wanted to do over. So many things he yearned to change. Nevertheless, history stared at him like an adamant stone, unyielding to his personal desires, unmoved by his contrition. "If we hadn't gone looking for fuel, Mom would still be here. If we hadn't taken on Hammer, Dad would still be alive. Maybe I should stop while I'm ahead. Perhaps I can talk Eric and Jimmy into stepping down. They're sensible men. They'll know that this fight will never end."

He continued whispering his manifesto of defeat to himself. "Either way, my struggle is over. To continue could mean losing Cole. It could cost Julianna her life. Even though she isn't mine, I can't stand the thought of her being gone. I can't imagine Cole growing up in this heartless world without a mother."

He sat alone in the darkness for a while longer. The flames died low. The glowing embers competed with the fading blaze, both dwindling in the cool night air.

"Shane?"

Only one voice left on earth had the power to revive him from the depths of utter despair to which he'd sank. He turned to look at her.

Julianna took the seat vacated by Cole and dried her hair with a towel. She combed it out with her fingers. "Are you going to bed soon?"

"I don't know."

"Big day tomorrow. You should get some rest."

"Big day how?"

"We have to figure out how we're going to take down Hammer."

He gave a sigh of vanquishment. "Maybe we

should let it go. Admit that we've been beaten."

"Excuse me?" She craned her neck to look into his eyes. "Shane, I realize that you're hurting. You've lost both of your parents, your childhood home, and your fiancé in a matter of months. But this is no time to give up. You still have a lot to fight for."

"Like what?"

"Like your son!"

"He's exactly the reason I think we should consider giving in to Hammer's demand. We can't win. We have no idea where he's hiding, nor how many men he has with him. The more we press him, the more he'll push back."

She took his hand. "Your father was the one who started this movement, to stand up to Jack PAC, to refuse to exist as serfs under the subjugation of Hayes and Hammer. When Paul died, everyone looked to you to continue the charge. So far, you've been faithful. You picked up his mantle and you're growing into the kind of leader that people will follow. Yes, Eric is the sheriff, and Jimmy is the mayor, but even they come to you for advice and counsel.

"Too many eyes are on you for inspiration. If you keep fighting or if you give up, a lot of people are going to follow your example. This isn't just about you, or me, or Cole."

Had these words come from anyone else, they would have fallen on deaf ears. They would have been as the ashes in the fire before him.

Julianna stirred the coals. She put a few more sticks of wood on the waning cinders. She broke up a few small twigs of tinder on the glowing coals. Soon, the fire rekindled, providing light, warmth, and a frail glimmer of hope.

She sat near him for the next hour, as if keeping a vigil for all that had been lost. Neither said anything but simply gazed on the dancing flames. Finally, she hugged him. "I'm going to turn in. You should go to bed soon, also. And think about what I said."

He patted her on the hand before she left. "Thank you. I will."

CHAPTER 25

Arise, O Lord; save me, O my God: for thou hast smitten all mine enemies upon the cheek bone; thou hast broken the teeth of the ungodly.

Psalm 3:7

Thursday morning, Shane pulled into the Teague family compound. He cut the ignition and looked over to Julianna. "I wish I could convince you to sit this one out."

"I feel like we've had this conversation before." She opened the door and exited the truck.

Shane opened his door, stepped out, and turned to see Bobby's pickup pulling in behind the Ram. Bobby, Pastor Joel, and Dan poured out of the second vehicle. He closed the door and led the way up the steep hill to the barn beside James Teague's home.

Once inside, Shane and his team joined the others who were gathered around an old wooden stake-bed wagon. James stood at the head of the wagon, flanked by his sons, Jimmy and Johnny. Sheriff Bivens and Butterbean stood on the side. All faced in, as if at a large, stand-up, boardroom table.

Eric Bivens had been speaking when Shane and the others arrived. "Finding Hammer is the hard part. The best we can hope for right now is that he'll strike again, and we can tail his arsonist back to the camp."

Jimmy shook his head. "That's gonna be like splitting hickory with a butter knife, Sheriff."

"Have you got a better idea, Mr. Mayor?" asked Bivens.

"No, but sitting around and waiting, trying to guess where he'll strike next is no plan at all," Jimmy replied.

"My brother will know where Hammer is staying," said Pastor Joel.

"The hard part will be convincing him to tell us," added Bobby.

"If he knows, he'll tell us," said Shane. "I can make sure of that."

Dan asked, "How do you know he's telling us the truth? If you put the screws to him, he might tell you anything you want to hear just to get the pain to stop."

Shane felt the anger over his mother's and father's deaths, the hostility over his childhood home being destroyed. It percolated inside him like acid. "I'll make sure he never wants to see my face again when I'm done with him. I'll make sure he knows that if I have to come back and ask again, I'll bring ten-fold the pain and agony he suffered during the first interview."

Johnny Teague's face looked concerned. "Maybe it would be better if someone else questioned him. You might be too close to this one, Shane. I don't have any sympathy for Wallace Hayes, but if you let your emotion get the better of you, he could die. Then, our best source of information will be gone."

Pastor Joel studied the weathered and pitted surface of the old wagon. "He's my brother. As awful of a person as he is, I don't want to see him die. But even so, I know him like no one else does." The pastor looked up at Shane. "Seeing the fury in Shane's eyes, he'll tell us what he knows. He's a ruthless man, but he can still be motivated by fear. I believe Shane should be the one to question him. He'd be a fool to hold out on Shane." The pastor turned to Jimmy. "Whatever you want to say about my brother, he's no fool."

"How do we know Wallace Hayes isn't in on this?" Julianna looked around at the men in the barn.

Jimmy shook his head. "I seriously doubt it. After Hayes stepped aside and didn't support Hammer with the raid at the elections, I think the two of them parted ways."

"Then why do we think Hayes is going to know where Hammer is hiding out?" she asked.

"He might not know exactly, but he'll have an

idea of where we can start looking," said the pastor.

"Let's take a ride up there." Vexed by his loss, Shane was anxious to get this hunt started. "It won't hurt anything to ask."

Johnny grabbed his rifle and looked at his brother. "You should hang back. This is Wallace Hayes we're talking about. He may require some unconventional interrogation techniques. It would be best if you didn't risk sullying the mayor's office over this." He glanced at Bivens. "You, too, Sheriff. We'll take a radio along and call you if we need you."

Bivens didn't seem to like being asked to sit on the sidelines. He crossed his arms and the corners of his mouth turned down. "Bobby, I'm counting on you and Johnny to keep a short leash on Shane. Don't let him take it too far."

Bobby put his hand on Shane's shoulder as he followed him out of the barn. "We'll take care of him."

Johnny paused on the way out the door. "Dad, you and Jimmy should get the wives and grandchildren ready. Take them out to the hunting cabin. Once we find Hammer, it's going to be a firestorm."

Shane waited for him. "Eric, get your men ready. When we get a location, we need to put together a plan and hit him fast."

"I'm not going to drag my feet on this, Shane. You can count on that," said Bivens.

Shane nodded and motioned for his team to follow him. "Dan, you ride with Julianna and me. You know the way up there better than anyone.

Pastor Joel, you, too. Maybe you can convince your brother to talk to us without the situation devolving into World War III."

***

Thirty minutes later, Shane raced up the driveway to the mountain retreat home of Wallace Hayes.

"You better slow your roll," warned Dan. "We don't know what we're walking into."

"Last time it was just me, you, and Butterbean. Hayes had an entire security team. We waltzed right in there," Shane replied.

"Yeah, well, as them investment types say, past performance may not be indicative of future results." Dan readied his rifle for a fight.

"Listen to him," said Julianna. "Dan is right. You're emotional."

"I think I've earned the right to be."

"I'm not arguing against that," she said. "But you can't let it interfere with your decision-making process. Slow down. Think it through. If you rush this and more people you care about get killed, you'll regret it. I know how you are."

Shane considered her words. If Julianna were to be injured, he'd most definitely blame himself. "Yeah, okay. I'll take it easy." He glanced over to Dan. "Thanks, buddy."

"I'm here to help."

Shane called Bobby over the radio. "The house is just up ahead. We'll roll up first to see how we're received. If you hear shooting, that means we need help. Otherwise, give us two minutes before you come in."

"A lot can happen in two minutes. How about we make it one?"

Shane agreed, "Okay. One."

He rolled to a stop when a tall, lanky guard walked out in front of the pickup with his hand in the air. The guard wore civilian clothes, but Shane recognized him as Officer Hicks, the man Bobby enjoyed referring to as Lurch.

"You need to turn your vehicle around. You're on private property." Lurch held his rifle low.

Shane looked at the single other guard standing at the side of the driveway. He rolled down his window. "Mr. Hicks, I thought you had house privileges. I'm guessing that if you've been forced to work the entrance gate, Wallace's security detail is pretty thin."

"I said turn your vehicle around!" Hicks put both hands on his rifle and looked at the other guard.

Shane glared at the pale man. "I came up here to speak with Wallace Hayes. If we turn around, that only means I'm going to let myself in the back door instead of knocking on the front. I promise, things will get a whole lot messier if I have to resort to plan B. Do you think your employer has the staff to thwart a stealth attack coming in from every side of the forest? He certainly didn't last time I was here. You might want to speak with him before we turn around."

Hicks studied Shane as if to decide whether he might be bluffing.

Shane picked up the radio. "Bobby, come on up

here, nice and slow. Lurch needs a little help to make the right call."

Bobby's F-150 climbed the gravel drive and stopped right behind Shane.

Shane watched Lurch's gray eyes shift from vehicle to vehicle. "If we have to come back later, your odds of survival go down tremendously."

Lurch frowned. He removed the radio from his belt and walked away from Shane so he couldn't hear his conversation. Moments later, Lurch returned. "Mr. Hayes will see you, but no guns."

Shane tightened his jaw. "That's not his call. I'm coming in and I'm bringing my guns. The only question is if I get an invitation and keep things pleasant, or if I have to kill every one of you and raze this house to the ground!"

"He's just lost his mother and his home," said Julianna. "It wouldn't be wise to push him."

Lurch looked away. "Pull through."

Shane and Bobby both drove their trucks up to the house. Everyone rolled out of the vehicles. Lurch and the other guard walked up from the gate, leaving their post and confirming Shane's notion that the compound was scarcely secured.

Wallace Hayes came outside holding a long-barrel revolver. "What do you want?"

"I want to talk. Let's go inside."

"We can talk outside," said Hayes.

"We're going inside. Have your men put down their weapons."

"Absolutely not!"

Shane swung the butt of his rifle up and struck Hayes in the lip, causing him to drop the pistol.

Bobby and Julianna quickly drew on Lurch. Dan and Johnny drew on the other guard. The two men lowered their weapons and Pastor Joel collected the firearms from each of the men.

Shane glared at Hayes. "This is not a negotiation. I'm here to talk to you. If you tell me what I want to know and do things my way, you can live through this. Otherwise, your wife will be mopping up blood. I'll leave this place just like I did the last time I was here."

He grabbed Hayes by his collar and pushed him toward the entrance. "Get inside!"

Hayes opened the door. The entire entourage followed him in.

"Daddy!" Evelyn stood near the entrance, leaning on her forearm crutches. "Why are they here again?"

Gina stood behind her daughter. Her lip quivered.

"Just go to the bedroom with Mama, Sweet Pea," said Hayes.

Evelyn had little control of her expression, but Shane could sense the disdain she felt for him. Her chin wavered left to right until her eyes met Shane's. "You act like Daddy is the bad guy and you're some shining knight on a white horse. But you're the monster!" She pivoted on her crutches and followed her mother to the bedroom.

Shane felt awful for terrorizing the young girl once again. But he had to keep moving forward. "Julianna, go with Gina and Evelyn. Make sure they don't have any weapons back there." He watched as Bobby and Dan finished putting restraints on Lurch and the other guard.

He looked at Hayes. "Do you have any other guards in the house we should know about?"

Hayes said nothing.

Shane punched him in the gut. "Last chance. Next time I have to ask twice, I'm going to start making a mess."

Hayes kept his eyes low. "The night shift guys, they're sleeping in the basement. Two of them."

"Bobby, take Dan and Johnny down there. Wake them up, hog tie them, and bring them upstairs." Shane motioned for Hayes and the others to walk to the living area.

Pastor Joel spoke to his brother. He explained what Harvey Hammer had done, burning down the house and killing Shane's mother.

Wallace Hayes looked up. "Shane, I didn't have anything to do with that!"

"You better pray that I don't find out different." Shane's eyes narrowed. "Where is Hammer camped out?"

"I don't know."

Shane took his knife from his front pocket, flicked it open, and drove it into Hayes' thigh, just above the knee.

Hayes screamed in torment. Shane withdrew the blade and wiped the blood on Hayes' pant leg. "You better start guessing. This isn't going to get any easier."

"Shane!" Hayes gasped for breath. "Are you crazy? Stop it!"

"If you want me to stop, you better tell me something I can work with." Shane held the blade to

Wallace's neck.

"Okay! Okay. Okay. Put that thing away, and I'll talk!" Hayes' voice quaked. His eyes were opened as wide as saucers. Beads of sweat formed on his forehead. "Just let me think!"

Bobby, Dan, and Johnny returned with the other guards, their hands also in restraints.

"Dan, you and Johnny check the rest of the house. Make sure we don't have any surprises."

The two searched the house while Shane continued his interrogation.

Wallace Hayes nodded. "Jackson Construction was working on an office building up in Balsam."

Shane cut him off. "An office building in Balsam." He threatened him with the knife. "Do I look stupid to you? Why would anyone build an office building in Balsam? There's nothing up there!"

Hayes closed his eyes and winced at the menacing blade so close to his cheek. "Wait, wait, wait! Just hear me out."

"This better be good," said Shane.

"It was never supposed to be occupied." Hayes looked at his brother then to Shane. "It was built as a paper loss. We bought the property from another shell corporation that we owned at an inflated price. We doctored the books to show more labor than we actually paid out, higher material costs, tax write-offs, you know."

"You mean tax evasion." Shane crossed his arms.

"Wasn't there a fire out there?" asked the pastor.

Hayes lowered his gaze. "There may have been."

Pastor Joel nodded. "I bet it was insured for the higher materials cost and I bet Jackson Construction or one of your little shell companies got the contract for the repairs."

Shane looked at the pastor. "So you know where this place is?"

"I have a general idea of the location. A dirt road out by Dark Ridge Creek."

"The road is paved now," Hayes said sheepishly.

The pastor added, "I'm sure Jackson Paving got that job."

"Do you have a plat map of the property?" Shane asked.

"Probably." Hayes pointed to a door near the entrance. "In my study."

Shane and the pastor escorted the slippery swindler while Bobby kept an eye on Lurch and the other guards. Wallace Hayes instructed them which drawers to check for the plans.

Dan and Johnny returned and peeked into the office. "The rest of the house is clear," said Johnny.

"Good." Shane took the maps and drawings. "Let's get going. This seems to be our best option."

Shane grabbed some of the rifles on his way out the door. "Julianna, we're rolling out," he yelled. "Scoop up the rest of their weapons," he said to Bobby and the others.

"You can't take all of our guns!" said Hayes.

"Why not?" asked Shane. "You took all of mine, remember? Besides, I'm guessing you've got more stashed somewhere. Also, if we don't find Hammer, I'll be back. I don't want these being used on me during my next visit."

"Should we cut them loose?" asked Bobby.

"Gina seems capable of working a pair of scissors. It will lower our chances of being shot in the back," said Shane.

Julianna emerged from the back room. "Do we know where he's at?"

"We have a pretty good idea. Come on." Shane led the group back to the vehicles.

CHAPTER 26

It is God that avengeth me, and subdueth the people under me. He delivereth me from mine enemies: yea, thou liftest me up above those that rise up against me: thou hast delivered me from the violent man.

Psalm 18:47-48

Thursday afternoon, Shane loaded magazines into the front of his tactical vest. The Teague family compound buzzed with energy. It served as the staging area for the assault on the potential location of Harvey Hammer's lair. Julianna, Bobby, Dan, and Pastor Joel likewise readied themselves for the coming engagement.

"I'm asking for volunteers for the recon team."

Sheriff Bivens approached Shane's group.

Shane wrinkled his forehead. "Recon team?"

"Yeah, I want to take in four or five guys to see what we're dealing with."

"You'll risk tipping our hand." Shane shook his head. "We should just go in hard and fast. For all we know, Hayes could have informed Hammer about our intent as soon as we left."

"In which case, we need to know what we're walking into," said the sheriff.

"Sounds like a waste of time, if you ask me." Shane scowled.

Pastor Joel said, "We're all anxious to eliminate this threat, but I think we need to listen to the sheriff. He's trained for this sort of thing."

Shane looked at Dan and Bobby for support but got none. "Fine. If you're determined to send in a recon team, I'll go."

"Me, too," said Julianna.

"I'm in," echoed Bobby.

Dan nodded. "I'll come along if you need me."

Bivens looked at Dan's leg. "You still have a little limp. Why don't you save your strength for the main event?" He turned to the pastor. "You, too. I don't want to risk irritating your shoulder wound before the battle starts. Volunteers, come with me."

Shane followed Bivens to his vehicle. "What about everyone else? When will you bring them in?"

"I'm not sure, but it's my call. I'll have them stationed at the rally point about a mile out, down by Willets-Ochre. If we need them, they can get to us in a matter of minutes." Bivens reached his SUV.

"A mile out? If Hammer spots us, he'll have no trouble melting into the forest. Then we'll never track him down."

"That's a risk I'm willing to take," said the sheriff. "Walking into a situation that I know nothing about isn't."

Shane sulked. "That's because you're underestimating the price of letting him get away. Hammer will be a thorn in our side until the day someone puts a bullet in his skull."

"I appreciate your concern, but like I said, this is my operation. We're going to do it my way." Bivens turned his back to Shane and shook hands with Johnny Teague. "You're joining us?"

"It's the only way I could get my stubborn brother to stay home. He doesn't seem to grasp the continuity-of-government concept."

"Yeah, we need him to be safe." Bivens unfolded a map of the Balsam area. "If something bad happens to the mayor, our fledgling local government will crumble."

Studying the map, the five of them reviewed the location of the office building in the woods. "Johnny and I will hike the road in, keeping to the cover of the woods. Shane, you'll take your team in the back way. You can follow Dark Ridge Creek along here." The sheriff traced the path with his finger.

"Once we've got eyes on everyone, you'll bring in the troops?" asked Shane.

"If we like what we see, yes. I need to know what kind of security Hammer has on the entrance road. That's going to be our primary avenue of approach."

"What do you mean by, if you like what you see?" Shane quizzed.

"I mean, if we can't get in there and do our job without losing a lot of our people, we'll scrub the assault and come back."

Shane shook his head. "We can't let this monster live."

Julianna, Bobby, and Johnny added nothing to the debate.

Bivens raised his hand. "I don't intend to. We'll come back, use the information we gather from the reconnaissance mission, and formulate a new plan."

Shane tightened his jaw. "Giving Hammer time to slip away like a snake."

"It is what it is, Shane," said Johnny. "This is what the sheriff wants to do and it's how we're going to play it."

"Okay." Shane threw his hands in the air. "Let's get this show on the road."

Bivens called over his radio. "All team leaders, get your people ready to move out to the rally point. Once there, stay on high alert until I call you into assault position or cancel the operation."

Shane made no attempt to hide his disappointment. "I'll have Pastor Joel drop us off at the creek and take the truck back to the rally point."

***

Pastor Joel prayed for Shane, Bobby, and Julianna before dropping them off where Dark Ridge Creek crossed the road. "Lord, watch over this team. Keep 'em safe. Amen."

"Thanks." Shane stepped out of the truck and closed the door.

Julianna and Bobby followed him into the woods and up the brook.

Heavy spring undergrowth covered the forest floor. In many places, Shane had no other choice but to walk through the shallow stream of water.

"Wait!" Julianna whispered.

Shane turned to see that she'd been caught up in a tangle of briars. He stopped to help her step free from the brambles. "This will be a terrible path for a retreat if things get dicey."

Bobby gingerly held back one of the canes of thorns for Julianna. "Any obstacles we have to go through, they will, too."

"Yes, but I'd rather be the one chasing someone through a briar patch than the one being chased." Julianna finally got clear of the impediment and continued following Shane through the dense brush.

After following the stream for roughly a quarter mile, Shane led the team away from the brook. "This hill looks like a good place to climb. We should be able to see the structure from the top."

Once on the crest of the incline, Shane took out his binoculars. "That's it!" He observed the large, concrete block structure. It was finished, with a roof, windows, and a paved parking lot, but the property looked almost ridiculous in the middle of nowhere. He pressed the talk key on the encrypted radio. "I count six vehicles in the parking lot. I see two guys with rifles hanging out by the front door." Shane watched for a moment. "It looks like they're passing a joint!"

Bivens' voice returned over the secure frequency. "No one watching the perimeter on this side. We didn't see any surveillance on the road in either. I didn't spot any cameras but that doesn't mean there aren't some concealed in the trees. Are you able to observe any activity inside the building?"

"Two of the offices have lights on inside. One has four guys sitting at a table. I just saw someone walk by the window of the other. It looks like a total of eight units. Why don't you bring in the troops and we can split up into eight teams? Each of us will clear one office."

"I don't know, Shane. Something about this doesn't sit right with me." The sheriff paused, then said, "Hammer is no idiot. He wouldn't leave his compound so lightly guarded."

"Since he knows you're likely to be involved, he would probably assume that you'd stage a pre-dawn raid. Isn't that protocol for the sheriff's department?" asked Shane.

"Yes, but that's when he'd most expect us. I'd never hit him then. He must know that. Have you identified him from among any of the men inside?"

"No, but I can't make out faces from this distance," Shane replied. "I understand your reasoning, but whatever he thinks, obviously he's not expecting us right now. The other explanation is that he's down to stoners and thugs for his army. Perhaps we overestimated his numbers. Could have been a schism in the camp. Maybe some of his lackeys split off, formed their own gang. You told me that Jacob Van Burren brought in a bunch of his low-life comrades to help Hammer maintain control. I could envision that relationship ending poorly."

"That's all possible, but it's just speculation," said the sheriff. "I want to take this discussion back to the compound. I want the mayor to weigh in on this. We'll hash it out and decide what to do tomorrow."

"No!" Shane immediately realized he'd spoken too loudly. He lowered his voice and repeated his response. "No! These guys are sitting ducks! This is our golden opportunity. I'm not walking away from this!"

"It's not your call."

"I don't work for the sheriff's department. You can't tell me what to do." Shane looked back at Bobby and Julianna. He pressed the talk key again. "Dan, Pastor Joel, can you guys each take charge of a group of civilian troops? Bivens is backing out but we're going in. My team will commence the assault in five minutes. We'll snipe off the two guards, then start advancing toward the main structure. When you get here, start clearing the offices beginning with the one closest to the road." Shane took aim at one of the stoners tasked with keeping watch. "Bobby you take the one on the left."

Dan replied, "I'll do whatever you need me to do, Shane. Pastor Joel is with you, too. But for the record, we both believe it would be better if we all stuck together."

"I agree, but we've got him in the crosshairs. If we let him slip away, we may never get another shot," said Shane.

"That's why we're with you," said Dan.

"I'll start punching holes in that window where they're all sitting around the table," said Julianna.

Bivens' voice came over the radio. "Shane! It doesn't work like this. Either we're all in or we're all out."

"You do what you have to do and I'll do what I have to do." Shane checked his watch. "This operation will commence in four minutes."

"You're forcing my hand." Bivens' voice sounded angry.

"I'm forcing nothing. You're free to do whatever you want," said Shane. "And so am I."

One minute later, the sheriff's voice came over the radio once more. "Johnny and I are coming to you. I'll have my deputies come all the way to the parking lot. Watch out for them."

"Don't do me any favors," said Shane. "I'm running my team. If you're coming here, you're going to back us up, no questions."

"No questions—this time," replied Bivens. "But this is the last sheriff's operation you'll ever be involved with."

Shane didn't press the talk key, so Bivens didn't hear his reply. "That's fine by me." He took aim at the man taking the last short toke from his dwindling joint.

Bivens ordered his men to advance to the building over the radio.

Two minutes later, Julianna said, "Here they come."

"Right on time." Shane looked at Eric Bivens

and Johnny Teague working their way through the woods. "You two, pick a target in that center window. On one. Five, four, three, two …"

CHAPTER 27

For man also knoweth not his time: as the fishes that are taken in an evil net, and as the birds that are caught in the snare; so are the sons of men snared in an evil time, when it falleth suddenly upon them.

Ecclesiastes 9:12

Shane heard the rifles snap all at once. The two guards fell to the ground. The men sitting at the table in the office met their demise behind the shattered window. "Let's go!" Shane led the charge down the hill toward the building.

The sound of vehicles storming up the road preceded a cavalcade of sheriff's deputies racing to join the assault. Shane pointed to the office with the broken glass. "We'll start with that one!"

"Watch out!" yelled Bivens.

Shane looked to see two more men coming out of the other office where he'd seen a light. He slid behind a tree and exchanged fire with them. The others also got low to avoid being shot. Rounds flew back and forth until eventually, a phalanx of deputies made a run for the office where the shots had originated. "Clear!" yelled one of the deputies after gaining entry.

"Let's go!" Shane resumed his mission, sprinting headlong toward the office with the broken glass. He pulled the door open, raised his weapon and searched each room of the suite. "They were the only ones here."

Shane kept his rifle ready and led the team back to the door. He stuck his head out to see deputies coming out of the other office suites. "Anything?"

"All clear," replied one.

Another declared, "Same here."

Bivens inspected the slain men lying around the table. "I don't recognize any of these men. None of them are Van Burren or Hammer."

Butterbean entered the room. "Maybe Hammer has another crew out raiding for supplies."

Pastor Joel and Dan stood in the doorway. Pastor Joel said, "Or he could have…"

His statement was interrupted by heavy automatic gunfire. Shane turned toward the shattered window to see bright bursts of red and orange muzzle flash illuminating from the forest. "Get down!" He instinctively grabbed Julianna and tackled her to the floor. Blood splashed into his eyes. He cleared it with the sleeve of his shirt. "Are you hit?"

"No, I don't think so," she said.

The gunfire continued. Large projectiles ripped through the concrete blocks raining cement, shrapnel, and gray dust upon everyone in the room. Shane turned his head to see Pastor Joel lying right beside him. He stared into the pastor's eyes hoping for some encouraging word. None came. Neither did the man's eyes blink when bullets sent more debris falling down on his face. "Pastor Joel?"

No answer came. Shane quickly realized it had been the pastor's blood which had sprayed all over his face at the onset of the counterassault.

Eric Bivens crawled on his stomach to a more interior room. He put out a call over the radio. "This is an ambush! If you can get to a vehicle and get away, do it! Go now!"

Shane looked outside to see several civilians and deputies scuttling toward the vehicles. He watched helplessly as most were cut down indiscriminately by the heavy machine gun. The sickening realization that he was to blame caused his skin to flush. He felt cold, clammy, undone by a sensation akin to walking off of a cliff by accident. "Oh, no! What have I done?" He felt a tug at his tactical vest.

"Y'all need to get away from the door." Bobby dragged Shane and Julianna further back into the office.

The gigantic projectiles continued to rip through the walls overhead for what seemed like a lifetime. "What are they shooting?" asked Johnny with a petrified look on his face.

"Browning M2, probably." Eric Bivens kept his head down and his hands on his rifle. "Fifty cal."

"Any idea where they're at?" asked Dan.

"I saw flashes coming from the woods, but I couldn't see the shooter," Shane replied.

Soon, the deafening fusillade ceased.

"Follow me to the door!" Shane crawled back to the entrance. "Stay out of the windows!"

Bivens kept close to him as did Bobby.

Shane looked through his scope. "They were right over there."

"I don't see anyone!" Bobby complained.

"Come on out with your hands up," called a voice over a bullhorn.

"That's Hammer," said Bivens.

The bullhorn continued, "In case you're a little slow in figuring things out, you folks put your feet right in the middle of a bear trap. We've got enough ammo to turn this entire structure into a rock pile. I know what you're thinking. They'd never do that to their own investment property. But as it turns out, we were having a little trouble renting it out anyhow. Real estate really is all about location, location, location. Live and learn, I guess."

Shane looked up to see a section of the wall collapse onto the floor. Part of the wall to the next office suite came down also, leaving a seven-foot-wide orifice in the front of the building. "If we can't see our target, we don't have a chance."

"I'm afraid they've dug into the side of the hill, like a pillbox or something." Bivens continued to try looking out.

"If we give up, he'll kill us anyway," Julianna

lay on her stomach behind Shane.

Shane looked over the heavily perforated structure. "One more sustained volley like the last one, and he'll bring the walls down on top of us. We'll be buried alive." He'd already killed so many people by his impetuous thirst for revenge. Shane could not bear to watch Julianna die because of his mistake. "I think we're going to have to give up."

Julianna's eyes filled with tears. "No, Shane. This will be worse than death."

If she weren't there, he'd pick up his rifle and charge into the woods. He sighed. "I'm sorry."

"Shane is right. We have to throw in the towel," said Bivens.

"I'm sorry to you, too," said Shane.

Bivens shook his head and forced a smile. "I knew your emotions were raw. Your home was burned to the ground, your mother killed, and you've not even had one single day to process it. I should have never allowed you to take part in this action."

"You couldn't have stopped me."

"I could have. And I should have. I could have assigned two deputies to sit on you until we wrapped this thing up. Don't blame yourself, Shane. You wanted justice for your mother, your father, and your home. Anyone who's been through what you have would've acted exactly the same way. It's my fault for not shutting it down."

Shane smiled at his friend. "Thanks for trying to make me feel better but…"

The bullhorn interrupted them. "I'm not going to ask again. Come out with your hands up, or I'm going to turn this place into a pile of gravel."

Shane removed the pistol from his tactical vest and placed it on the floor next to his rifle. He stood up and placed his hands on his head. "Julianna, come on."

Her lip quivered, but she complied, as did the others.

***

"You see this?" Harvey Hammer shoved the gold star badge into Eric Bivens' face. "I've always been the sheriff of Jackson County. You're just a wannabe. You don't have what it takes to be a leader." He looked around at Shane and the other hostages lined up against the walls with their hands secured behind their backs. Hammer took his radio. "Although, I will commend you on changing the encryption on the radios. I don't know how you did it, but you managed to block me out."

Jacob Van Burren and two of his henchmen stood behind Hammer, holding weapons.

Hammer pressed the talk key of Eric's radio. "Jimmy Teague, are you listening?"

A voice replied, "This is the mayor."

"Not for long, it ain't," laughed Hammer. "Listen here. I've got your brother, the sheriff, country music's golden boy, that pretty little gal he runs around with, and a few more of 'em tied up right here. Unless you want me to start sending them back to you piece by piece, you need to resign immediately. It needs to be just as much of a public spectacle as it was when you took office. You'll hand over the reins to Wallace Hayes."

"It's not going to happen," said Jimmy. "Besides, I think Hayes is done with politics."

"That sniveling little coward is done when I say he's done!" shouted Hammer. "He'll wear the hat, but I'll be calling the shots from here on out."

"You'll pay for this," said the mayor.

Harvey Hammer drew his long barrel, shiny revolver. He pointed it at Eric Bivens who closed his eyes tightly and turned away. He pulled the trigger and shot Bivens in the head. More blood splattered on Shane who was sitting right next to the sheriff. Julianna screeched in terror and began wailing.

Hammer pressed the talk key once more. "The sheriff just resigned. I think it would be best for all involved if you'd step aside also. Here, I'm going to let you talk to your brother. Ask him if he thinks I'm bluffing."

"Johnny, what's going on?" cried the mayor.

"He just shot Eric in the head. They cut down more than three-quarters of the deputies in the ambush. We're in bad shape over here."

The mayor was quiet for some time. "If I step aside, you'll let them go?"

"If you step aside, I'll let them live. Where and how will be up to me." Hammer released the talk key.

"Okay, I'll get in touch with Hayes. We'll work out a public inauguration."

"I want a formal apology as well. And make it sound good. Remember, where and how your brother lives is up to me." Hammer smiled at his captives.

"Done," replied Jimmy. "I'll let you know when."

Hammer winked at Julianna. "I hope this all works out and I don't have to kill you. I've got big plans for you and me."

She shuddered and looked at Shane. "Why didn't you just let me die?"

Once again, he blamed himself for another mistake that he could not take back.

Harvey Hammer holstered his weapon. "Jacob, have your boys get this mess cleaned up. Move our guests to the back-corner office. Cut those zip-tie restraints and replace them with handcuffs. You should be able to find several pairs of cuffs on the dead deputies outside. Any of the uniforms that aren't soiled, strip them off and distribute them. We're the legitimate authority in this county. Ain't no point in running around looking like a gaggle of goons."

"Yes, sir." Jacob Van Burren had a jail-ink tattoo of an AK-47 on his neck. He'd need more than a uniform to make him look like an official lawman.

"I'll have the boys bring up the RVs. Won't be no place fittin' to sleep in this rat hole. At least not until we get it patched up." Hammer kicked a chunk of concrete block out of his way. "Hopefully, we won't be hiding out like a bunch of escaped convicts much longer, anyhow."

CHAPTER 28

Why standest thou afar off, O Lord? why hidest thou thyself in times of trouble? The wicked in his pride doth persecute the poor: let them be taken in the devices that they have imagined. For the wicked boasteth of his heart's desire, and blesseth the covetous, whom the Lord abhorreth.

Psalm 10:1-3

Shane sat in the dust on the bare concrete floor of the office, his back against the wall, and his hands cuffed behind his back. He stared blankly at the pockmarks in the wall opposite of where he sat. His eyes darted from person to person, thinking about how he'd sealed the fate of Julianna and the others. *I failed them all*, he thought. *At least the charade is over. I'm not a big music star anymore. I'm not a leader like my dad. And I'll never be a father to Cole.* He glanced at Julianna. *She wanted me to prove that I'm a man. I've done exactly the opposite. I did the same thing I've always done. I ran after what I wanted with complete disregard to what it would mean for everyone else. Last time, it was fame, fortune, and wild women. This time, it was my lust for revenge.*

I've paid a price for my actions, but I deserve everything I get. The people around me, they do nothing yet they seem to get a double dose of the consequences. Julianna was right. I should have picked up my rifle and walked right out that door. Harvey Hammer would still be around, but at least I could have ended the reign of terror caused by Shane Black.

"Shane?" Butterbean interrupted his internal concerto of self-loathing.

He looked up, annoyed by the intrusion. Eager to get back to mentally flogging himself, he asked, "What is it, Butterbean?"

"I have a handcuff key in my boot. It's under my insole."

Shane became completely distracted from his endeavor of self-immolation by the unusual comment. However, it served more as a bewildering curiosity than a gleaming ray of hope. "Why would you have a handcuff key in your boot?"

"I've heard lots of stories of correctional officers being taken hostage by inmates. They're almost always restrained with their own handcuffs. I put it there shortly after I started working at the jail."

Shane thought about the prospects for a moment. "Even if we get out of the cuffs, we're still locked in an office with two armed guards at the door."

"At least we can die trying." Julianna lay on her stomach and rolled to Butterbean's feet. "Which boot?"

"The right one. I'm right-handed," he added.

"But you can't reach your boot with either hand." Dan pointed out the obvious.

"I know!" Butterbean seemed frustrated.

Shane watched Julianna struggle for a moment, then worked his way over to her for assistance. Finally, they got the boot off and extracted the key. Shane held her hand as his fingers searched frantically for the keyhole. He had no illusions about the odds for a successful escape, but perhaps God would grant him one last prayer. Maybe he could create enough of a diversion for Julianna to get free. Perhaps Cole could still grow up with his mother.

"I got it!" Shane's mood improved immensely when he heard the lock of Julianna's cuffs click.

She quickly freed herself from the other cuff and then released Shane. Julianna continued around the room, removing the restraints from Butterbean, Bobby, Dan, and Johnny.

Bobby rubbed his wrists. "We need weapons."

Dan gently pried a large chunk of concrete from the damaged wall. "Slap this across somebody's head and it's night night."

Shane extracted a second piece of busted cinder block. "If we could get this middle brick out, we'd almost have a hole big enough to crawl through."

"That's gonna make a lot of racket." Butterbean shook his head.

"Then we need something to make more racket," said Shane. "Julianna, when we give you the signal, start screaming and yelling, telling the guards that you have to use the bathroom. The rest of us will go to work on breaking out this block with the bigger chunks we've found."

"When they come in to take her to the bathroom, we'll be like the dog who finally caught the car," said Johnny.

"Maybe not." Shane developed his scheme further. "If they come in, everyone hold your hands behind your backs. As soon as one of us has a clear shot, whack! We'll bust him in the head with a piece of cement."

"Sounds like a plan!" said Bobby. "Three of us can work on the wall while the other two men keep watch of their reactions to Julianna's squawking."

Shane handed out the largest chunks of concrete that he could find. "Dan and I will watch the door. Butterbean, Bobby, and Johnny, you three work on the wall."

"What do we do when we get out?" Butterbean asked.

Shane looked the team over. "We'll head south for an hour or so. Once we're sure we've lost them, we'll cut west. Eventually, we have to hit the river. We can figure out how to get home from there."

Julianna looked deep into his eyes. "Then this will have all been for nothing. Pastor Joel, Eric, all of those deputies, they all died for nothing."

"We're in no position to fight. Whether we're able to escape with our lives remains to be seen. But anything more is an absolute impossibility."

She continued presenting her case. "What if we were able to make it to one of those pill boxes? If they still have the .50 cal machine guns mounted inside, we could catch Hammer in his own trap."

"That's a big if." Shane's brow became heavily furrowed.

Butterbean seemed concerned. "What if the pill boxes are guarded?"

Shane dismissed the objection. "They're pointed in. Those bunkers were set up specifically to ambush us. They serve no purpose for defense. Hammer will be watching to see if the mayor tries to pull off a rescue mission. He'll move the guns out of there eventually, but it sounds like he's more concerned with getting camp set up for tonight." Shane looked at Julianna. "Can you shoot a .50 cal?"

"It pretty much looks like spray and pivot," she said. "From the looks of how they used them on us, it's not a surgical instrument that requires a master's degree to operate."

"Maybe not, but what about the reload?" Shane inquired.

"It's real easy," added Dan. "I went to a machine gun shoot in Kentucky once. You've got a little latch near the rear sight that opens the top flap. You lay the first shell at the front of that compartment, close the top flap, and hit the charging handle a couple of times."

Shane nodded. "Bobby, do you think you could

figure that out?"

"If it's as easy as Dan makes it sound."

Shane knew the strategy was a risky proposition, but if they didn't finish the job, Hammer had a good chance of catching up with them once they got away. "Good, then Bobby will come with us. Dan, Johnny, and Butterbean will try to get into the second pillbox. When we take out these two guards, each team will have one rifle."

"Hopefully a pistol as well," added Butterbean.

"Yeah, maybe." Shane looked at Julianna. "Are you ready?"

She nodded hesitantly. "Yeah, I think so."

"You can do it." He brushed his hand across her back. "Pitch the biggest fit you've ever thrown."

Julianna kicked the door. "Hey! I need to use the restroom!"

"Quiet down in there!"

She continued kicking wildly, banging louder and louder. The commotion provided excellent cover for the noise being made by Butterbean, Bobby, and Johnny who were feverishly chipping away at the center block. "Come on! I have to go now!"

"Pipe down! I have to call the boss and see how we're supposed to handle this!" yelled the guard.

"I can't wait, open up! Let me out!" She kicked and banged.

"We can't even hear without that noise. Be quiet in there, or you'll never get out," said the guard.

She kept up her tantrum for several minutes.

"Hey! Cut it out! The other guy went to get you a bucket!"

"A bucket?" she protested. "I'm in here with five guys! I can't go in a bucket!"

"Then go in your pants! A bucket is all you're getting!"

She maintained her belligerence and outbursts.

"Stand back! Stand back away from the door!" called the guard finally.

"This is it!" Shane warned the men working on the wall.

With their hands behind their backs, Butterbean and Bobby stepped in front of the hole, obscuring it more than any of the others could have.

"Step back!" The door opened and the two guards came inside. One carried the bucket and the other held his rifle at low ready.

Shane swung his hand from behind his back and clocked the bucket carrier in the side of the face with a triangular shaped piece of concrete. The flesh from his temple to his ear ripped open, and the guard went down.

"Hey!" The other guard raised his rifle. Dan grabbed the barrel and pushed it down while Julianna grabbed his hand to prevent him from pulling the trigger, which would sound the alarm. Johnny smashed his piece of cement on the top of the guard's head and he tumbled to the ground.

"Is he dead?" asked Butterbean.

Shane couldn't be sure, so he beat the man's skull with five additional strikes before stripping him of his rifle. "Get their weapons and let's go!"

Johnny took the second rifle while Julianna found a pistol tucked in the waistband of the first guard.

"I got a knife!" exclaimed Butterbean.

"Good." Shane grabbed the radio from one of the guards and handed it to Johnny. He took the other walkie for himself and ushered the team through the hole. "Now, let's move!"

"I'm stuck!" cried Butterbean.

"That's not an option!" Shane shoved the big boy through the opening, then crawled out himself. He looked at Dan. "As soon as you get there, start shooting. Do like Hammer said, cave the roof down on the guards."

Dan nodded, then he, Johnny, and Butterbean headed into the woods toward the best estimate of where the bunker was located.

"Let's go!" Shane held the rifle, ready to engage but tried to keep to the trees without being spotted.

"That's it! I see the bunker over there!" Julianna whispered excitedly.

Shane led the way.

"It's completely unattended, just like you said." Bobby looked inside.

"Try to find a light." Shane opened several of the ammo boxes to have the shells ready to reload. "It's getting dark, and we'll have a tough time feeding a new belt into the top if we can't see."

Julianna stood behind the big gun.

The radio sprang to life. "Ken, did y'all get that bathroom situation addressed?" It was Hammer's voice.

"I found a flashlight!" said Bobby.

"Good." Shane waited to hear the next line of communications over the radio.

Hammer's voice came back. "Ken, pick up when

I call you."

Seconds later, he said, "Jacob, get some boys down there to the last office and see what's going on with the prisoners. Ken ain't responding."

"That's our cue." Shane patted Julianna on the back. "Light 'em up!"

Flashes of fire and deafening blasts echoed inside the simple dirt bunker made of sandbags, and wooden boards. Julianna quickly ripped through the first belt of ammo. Shane held the light while Bobby replaced the belt of linked ammunition. The sound of the second machine gun tearing through the camp could barely be heard over the ringing in Shane's ears.

Bobby slapped the top flap shut. "Go!"

Julianna continued her assault. Shane watched the carnage through the small opening between the sandbags. He kept the rifle near in case he saw anyone escape the bombardment and attempt to flank their location. The heavy bullets tore through the sides of the RVs like wet paper. The projectiles continued their destructive paths to the concrete walls.

After three more boxes of ammunition, the four RVs each resembled soda cans which had experienced the detonation of multiple cherry bombs. They were mangled beyond recognition. Parts of the building behind were crumbling like chalk in the fist of a gorilla.

"Keep it up! We have to take down those walls!" Shane handed the next belt to Bobby to load.

"I need a break." Julianna wiped the sweat from her forehead.

Shane took over and waited for Bobby to close the flap.

"Go!" said Bobby.

Shane opened up the big gun, hammering the remaining walls, which could still possibly provide concealment for his enemies. He continued through five more boxes of ammo.

"This thing is getting hot," said Bobby. "I don't see anything you could properly call a wall or surviving section of building."

Shane surveyed the rubble. "No, I don't suppose you could. Bobby, stay on the gun and give it a break. We'll go see if anyone needs a bullet in the head to get where they're going."

Julianna drew her pistol and followed Shane out the door.

"Shane?" Butterbean's voice came over the radio. "Are y'all okay?"

"Yes, good to hear your voice. We're coming out. Hold your fire."

Shane saw the mangled bodies of so many of Hammer's men. Most were far beyond the point of needing an extra bullet. Yet when he came across one still moving, he quickly dispatched the suffering fool.

Julianna picked up the first available battle rifle and tucked her pistol in her waist. She assisted in dispensing mercy upon the agonizing survivors. She kicked one to roll him over. "This looks like it could have been Van Burren."

Shane looked at the bloody mess. The face was gone, but he could still make out the butt of a rifle tattooed on the neck. "Yeah, probably was."

Shane rounded the corner where the office building had once been. His eyes locked with those of Harvey Hammer. There, lying in a soup of blood and rubble, was the man who'd killed his father, his mother, and burned down his home. His left leg was gone from just below the knee. His right arm ended at the wrist where a jagged bit of bone protruded from the red bits of skin and tendon. Deformed and disfigured by his own trap, Hammer maneuvered with his remaining hand and foot. He grunted and reached for a pistol laying nearby. Shane put his boot on the greedy fingers still determined to take one more life. The monstrous form no longer looked human, yet Shane felt no sympathy for the thing.

Julianna walked up behind him. "Are you going to do it?"

Shane wanted to. He itched inside to satisfy his desire for vindication. But he recalled where this lust had taken him before. He remembered what it had cost all those who'd followed him. "If I do it, it will be an act of revenge. I think you should be the one who pulls the trigger."

"Are you sure?" she asked.

The temptation to recant tugged at his innermost self. "Yeah, I'm sure."

She put the barrel of the rifle to Harvey Hammer's head. Hammer looked up at her, growled with an animalistic snarl. His teeth were red from his internal hemorrhaging.

POW! Shane watched the killer fall limp.

She stepped near to him. "That was a big thing you did."

"What?"

"Letting me kill Hammer when you wanted to be the one to do it. You're growing up, Shane Black. You're becoming a man."

The shame and regret of all his former sins still haunted him, but this single statement from Julianna did more to lift his spirits than anything else ever could have. With the tip of his boot, Shane rolled over what was left of Harvey Hammer onto his back. He bent down and retrieved the sheriff's badge from his front pocket. "Let's go home."

DON'T PANIC!

Inevitably, books like this will wake folks up to the need to be prepared, or cause those of us who are already prepared to take inventory of our preparations. New preppers can find the task of getting prepared for an economic collapse, EMP, or societal breakdown to be a source of great anxiety. It shouldn't be. By following an organized plan and setting a goal of getting a little more prepared each day, you can do it.

I always try to include a few prepper tips in my novels, but they're fiction and not a comprehensive plan to get prepared. Now that you're motivated to start prepping, the last thing I want to do is leave you frustrated, not knowing what to do next. So I'd like to offer you a free PDF copy of *The Seven Step Survival Plan.*

For the new prepper, *The Seven Step Survival Plan* provides a blueprint that prioritizes the different aspects of preparedness and breaks them down into achievable goals. For seasoned preppers who often get overweight in one particular area of preparedness, *The Seven Step Survival Plan* provides basic guidelines to help keep their plan in balance, and ensures they're not missing any critical segments of a well-adjusted survival strategy.

To get your **FREE** copy of ***The Seven Step Survival Plan***, go to **PrepperRecon.com** and click the FREE PDF banner, just below the menu bar, at the top of the home page.

Thank you for reading
Black Swan, Book Two: Carrion

Reviews are the best way to help get the book noticed. If you liked the book, please take a moment to leave a review on Amazon or Goodreads.

I love hearing from readers! So whether it's to say you enjoyed the book, to point out a typo that we missed, or asked to be notified when new books are released, drop me a line.
prepperrecon@gmail.com

Stay tuned to **PrepperRecon.com** for the latest news about my upcoming books.

Keep watch for
Black Swan, Book Three: Gehenna

Can't get enough post-apocalyptic chaos? Check out my other heart-stopping tales about the end of the world as we know it.

The Days of Noah

In an off-site CIA facility outside of Langley, rookie analyst Everett Carroll discovers he's not being told the whole truth. He's instructed to disregard troubling information uncovered by his research. Everett ignores his directive and keeps digging. What he finds goes against everything he's been taught to believe. Unfortunately, his curiosity doesn't escape the attention of his superiors, and it may cost him his life.

Meanwhile, Tennessee public school teacher, Noah Parker, like many in the United States, has been asleep at the wheel. During his complacency, the founding precepts of America have been systematically destroyed by a conspiracy that dates back hundreds of years.

Cassandra Parker, Noah's wife, has diligently followed end-times prophecy and the shifting tide against freedom in America. Noah has tried to avoid the subject, but when charges are filed against him for deviating from the approved curriculum in his school, he quickly understands the seriousness of the situation. The signs can no longer be ignored, and Noah is forced to prepare for the cataclysmic period of financial and political upheaval ahead.

Watch through the eyes of Noah Parker and Everett Carroll as the world descends into chaos, a global empire takes shape, ancient writings are fulfilled, and the last days fall upon the once-great United States of America.

Seven Cows, Ugly and Gaunt

Daniel Walker begins having prophetic dreams about the judgment coming upon America for rejecting God. Through one of his dreams, Daniel learns of an imminent threat of an EMP attack which will wipe out America's electric grid and most all computerized devices, sending the country into a technological dark age.

Living in a nation where all life-sustaining systems of support are completely dependent on electricity and computers, the odds of survival are dismal. Municipal water services, retail food distribution, police, fire, EMS and all emergency services will come to a screeching halt.

If they want to live, Daniel and his friends must focus on faith, wits, and preparation to be ready . . . before the lights go out.

Ava's Crucible

The deck is stacked against twenty-nine-year-old Ava. She's a fighter, but she's got trust issues and doesn't always make the best decisions. Her personal complications aren't without merit, but America is on the verge of a second civil war, and Ava must pull it together if she wants to survive.

The tentacles of the deep state have infiltrated every facet of American culture. The public education system, entertainment industry, and mainstream media have all been hijacked by a shadow government intent on fomenting a communist revolution in the United States. The antagonistic message of this agenda has poisoned the minds of America's youth who are convinced that capitalism and conservatism are responsible for all the ills of the world. Violent protest, widespread destruction, and politicians who insist on letting the disassociated vent their rage will bring America to her knees, threatening to decapitate the laws, principles, and values on which the country was founded. The revolution has been well-planned, but the socialists may have underestimated America's true patriots who refuse to give up without a fight.

Cyber Armageddon

Cyber Security Analyst Kate McCarthy knows something ominous is about to happen in the US banking system. She has a place to go if things get hectic, but it's far from the perfect retreat.

When a new breed of computer virus takes down America's financial network, chaos and violence erupt. Access to cash disappears and credit cards become worthless. Desperate consumers are left with no means to purchase food, fuel, and basic necessities. Society melts down instantly and the threat of starvation brings out the absolute worst humanity has to offer.

In the midst of the mayhem, Kate will face a post-apocalyptic nightmare that she never could have imagined. Her only reward for survival is to live another day in the gruesome new reality which has eradicated the world she once knew.

ABOUT THE AUTHOR

Mark Goodwin holds a degree in accounting and monitors macroeconomic conditions to stay up-to-date with the ongoing global meltdown. He is an avid student of the Holy Bible and spends several hours every week devoted to the study of Scripture and the prophecies contained therein. The troubling trends in the moral, social, political, and financial landscapes have prompted Mark to conduct extensive research within the arena of preparedness. He weaves his knowledge of biblical prophecy, economics, politics, prepping, and survival into an action-packed tapestry of post-apocalyptic fiction. Having been a sinner saved by grace himself, the story of redemption is a prominent theme in all of Mark's writings.

"He brought me up also out of an horrible pit, out of the miry clay, and set my feet upon a rock, and established my goings." Psalm 40:2

Made in the
USA
Lexington, KY